"Stop it, Owen. I know you don't want me and you probably don't need me."

Lulu pushed her nose at Brenna and she encircled her dog's neck to give her a big hug.

"Anyway," she continued, "it's probably just as hard on you to be around me all day. Every day."

"Brenna, my mother told me that you need to help run camp. You have reasons, but she wouldn't explain."

She swallowed and started to play with her fidget rings.

"I don't think I could live with myself if I didn't help an old friend in need." He lowered his voice. "We were friends once, weren't we?"

"We were. I hope we still are." She rested her hands on her lap and met his eyes. "So I guess you deserve an explanation." She blew out a breath as though she were about to tell him something important. Was she finally going to tell him why she blocked his calls ten years ago?

Heidi Main writes sweet inspirational romance novels set in small towns. Though she lives in central North Carolina's suburbs, she dreams of acreage and horseback riding, which is why her novels include wide-open ranches and horses. Before starting her writing career, Heidi worked with computers and taught Jazzercise. A perfect Saturday is lounging on the deck with her husband and watching the many birds in their backyard. Learn more about her books at www.heidimain.com.

Books by Heidi Main

Love Inspired

Triple C Ranch

A Nanny for the Rancher's Twins
A Family for the Orphans
The Farmer's Marriage Bargain

K-9 Companions

Her Loyal Companion
An Unexpected Texas Reunion

Visit the Author Profile page at LoveInspired.com.

AN UNEXPECTED TEXAS REUNION

HEIDI MAIN

LOVE INSPIRED

INSPIRATIONAL ROMANCE

LOVE INSPIRED®
INSPIRATIONAL ROMANCE

ISBN-13: 978-1-335-23033-1

Recycling programs for this product may not exist in your area

An Unexpected Texas Reunion

Love Inspired
22 Adelaide St. West, 41st Floor
Toronto, Ontario M5H 4E3, Canada
www.LoveInspired.com

HarperCollins Publishers
Macken House, 39/40 Mayor Street Upper,
Dublin 1, D01 C9W8, Ireland
www.HarperCollins.com

Printed in U.S.A.

I can do all things through Christ
which strengtheneth me.
—*Philippians* 4:13

To God be the glory.

Rich ~ thank you for supporting me through
this journey. Without you and your continuing
encouragement, I wouldn't have readers enjoying
my books today. I appreciate how you speak into
my life and build me up!

Shado ~ thank you for always being on the other
end of Messenger. Whenever I need farm or
country questions answered, you've got my back.
And when I have a word choice or paragraph or
scene that needs an extra set of eyes,
you are always on it. You have become invaluable
to my writing journey.

Chapter One

O wen McCaw leaned against the kitchen door-frame of his parents' home and swept back his four-month-old daughter's wispy hair. Evie was motherless because of him. He pressed his eyes closed, trying to block out the heart-wrenching phone call that had brought news of the car accident. Had he not worked overtime, Willow might still be alive. His stomach clenched that his thoughtlessness had forced his wife to drive herself to the baby shower. If he'd put work aside and gone home to pick her up, she might be alive today.

He took a deep breath of baby smell mixed with the formula Evie had just finished guzzling down and attempted to push the upsetting memories away. He ran a thumb along her jawline. His daughter ate like a linebacker and slept deeply, except for the times she was wide-awake in the middle of the night for hours at a time. He stared in awe at his precious child, then roughed a hand over his scruffy jaw. He still couldn't believe he was a single father now.

"Did she keep you up again last night?" his mother, Cora McCaw, asked, interrupting his musings as she hobbled on crutches and pulled out a skillet to make bacon. She'd fallen last week and broke her leg in two places, but had figured out those crutches real fast. Wait. Was his mother avoiding eye contact with him? Considering their past, he couldn't blame her. Regardless, being back at the Triple C Ranch in Serenity, Texas, made him feel like his feet were on solid ground for the first time since the fateful phone call. Four months had passed since the car accident had taken Willow and brought life to this little one.

"Maybe two hours. Other than that, she slept well." As the sizzling sound of bacon hit the air, he gazed at Evie. She startled, tensed and then relaxed again, the start of a smile on her heart-shaped lips. Delight swelled in his chest at how she'd so quickly wrapped him around her little pinkie.

"Can I help?" he asked as he set the spent bottle on the table. "Why don't you hold Evie and let me handle whatever you're doing?" His lengthy absence from the family hit him, sobering him. But a crisis usually brought clarity. And his wife's sudden death had done just that, making him wish he hadn't created such an uncomfortable chasm between him and his parents, especially his mother. He had so much to make up for.

She side-eyed him. "Owen, I can cook circles around you, even with crutches." She turned away quickly, but not before he saw her pained expression. "I wish…" she said, her voice barely audible "…well, I wish you had been more open to talking with us more over the years." Yep, lots to make up for.

"Mom, I'm so sorry," he muttered. But he knew words couldn't fix things between them. His mother's head bobbed as he sank into a kitchen chair. When he had called his parents to inform them of the accident, they had dropped everything and rushed to the hospital to be by Owen's side. He had greatly appreciated their presence, because in high school, he hadn't felt like his parents respected his decision to enter the military and then become a police officer, so he'd pushed them away. Hadn't accepted phone calls, and had ignored text messages, and when he did talk with them, it was mostly with grunts. Somehow, he'd gotten caught up in that childish behavior and had been unable to stop the cycle. So when they'd graciously invited him to come to the ranch to heal, he was pleasantly surprised and had accepted their offer readily.

"I appreciate you letting me move back in," he said. Their hospitality would allow him to take time to figure out what to do with his life, but it also seemed like the perfect time to rebuild his relationship with his parents.

His mother turned to him. "Owen. You are welcome here anytime, for as long as you want. Always have been." But he could see the sorrow in her eyes as regret lodged in his gut. The truth was, he'd hurt her.

"Thanks." He scuffed a hand over his face at his poor behavior over the years. He had to work his way back into their good graces. And he intended to do just that. The bacon's smoky scent lifted into the air, making his stomach growl.

"Do you have any ideas for your next step?" his mother asked as she moved the bacon to a paper towel.

"Is that a backhanded way of asking me about a time frame for when I'll get my own place?" He cringed at the ingratitude in his voice, especially when his mother's eyebrows rose. "I'm sorry," he said quickly to cover the words carelessly spoken. But the disappointment now spreading across his mother's face told him that a quick apology would not do. "I'm just frustrated the garage apartment isn't available." He kneaded the back of his neck where tension had gathered. That space would be perfect for him and Evie, as he was much too old to be living at home again.

His mother pushed the pile of luscious-smelling bacon toward him, then hobbled over and propped her crutches against the wall. She then settled in the chair next to him and placed a hand on his shoulder, her eyes glistening with emotion.

"I'm glad to have you home, Owen. Let's put the past where it belongs—in the past—shall we?" He gave her an appreciative nod, knowing it wouldn't be that easy, but he was willing to try. His mother turned her attention to Evie and gazed adoringly at her newest grandchild. At least his mother had someone worthy of her attention for the moment.

Two days ago, when his father had driven them under the familiar Triple C emblem, that feeling of being home had enveloped him. Now today, he appreciated that his mother was willing to overlook his failures. He selected three pieces of bacon and gobbled them down, his arm sweaty where Evie lay.

His mother leaned back and dug her fingers into the front of her cast and scratched. Or at least tried to. Her leg was so swollen there wasn't much space in there.

"I feel bad about your leg." She'd be on crutches for a minimum of six weeks so the tibia and fibula bones could properly heal.

She looked down at her cast, pulled out her fingers and chuckled. "I can't believe I broke my leg a week before camp starts." She scowled. Oh, yes, with everything that had happened with Willow and Evie's birth, he'd forgotten all about her summer camp. It was the first week of June, so camp was probably set to start on Monday. "I'm not sure what to do because I can't hobble around on crutches and be effective running camp."

Summer camp had been her baby for as long as he could remember. It had started as a one-week morning camp for younger kids who lived in Serenity, but over the years had grown to six weeks and included children in the surrounding areas. A morning session for the younger kids and the afternoon session for older ones. The children were taught how to plant vegetables and tend to them, about many different animals and how to care after them, as well as horseback riding and four wheeling. But the main reason his mother had started the camp was to share the gospel.

"If I could help, you know I would." His shrug had Evie's eyes briefly fluttering open. Oh, she wouldn't wake up. Not with the noise around her. She'd sleep most of the day and be up half the night as usual. He hugged her a little closer. Her unusual sleeping habits were fine because at night, when it was quiet, he had her all to himself. She would look at him with her big blue eyes like he was her hero. Well, she'd look at him differently when she learned the role he'd had in her mother's death. But for now, he enjoyed their middle-of-the-night adventures together. He might not be the best dad, but he loved spending time with his daughter.

His mother reached out and rubbed Evie's head. "Oh, that soft, downy hair. So precious," she whispered. He grinned at the two because it had only taken one afternoon with her newest grandchild—just long enough for Owen to take a ride around the ranch with his brother—to bond with Evie.

"What would you think about allowing me to watch the baby while you take my place at summer camp?"

Shock hit him like a ton of bricks. That she'd ask anyone to take her place was a surprise. But him? He smiled as his heart leaped with joy that she'd trust him with her summer camp. He had helped at the camp a lot as a kid, how hard could running it for six weeks be? As thorough as his mother was, it probably ran itself. Except, watching Evie wasn't a piece of cake. He glanced at his mother's crutches.

"I'm happy to help, but I thought you were supposed to have your leg elevated most of the day. And how are you going to get a bottle ready or carry Evie anywhere on crutches?"

His mother recommended he, or someone else, could come in every few hours and make up a bottle. And if his mother had everything she needed right around the couch and coffee table, then she wouldn't have to move Evie while standing.

"So the couch would be command central?" he joked.

"Exactly." His mother's eyes sparkled as though she were excited at the thought of watching her newest grandchild, then her expression grew concerned. "So I can count on you?" she said with a wary glance. A wave of regret washed over him for causing her to lose faith in him by behaving childishly over the years.

"Of course, Mom. I told you I'm back for good." He waited through the pregnant pause before his mother spoke again.

"Then it's settled." After they talked over a few more details, they agreed on the plan. His mother seemed almost relieved that he was willing to help. The fact that she'd trust him with her camp spoke volumes, right? Except simply running the camp for her would not restore their relationship. But it was a start. And he'd take it.

"Cora, you home?" a female voice called out.

"In here," his mother responded.

His breath caught in his lungs as his high school girlfriend—the last person he expected to see—walked in. She had broken his heart a decade ago before leaving town without a word.

A smile lit up Brenna Park's pretty face as she roughed up the fur of the dog beside her. Apparently, she hadn't noticed Owen.

He cocked his head and squinted at her in confusion. What was Brenna doing here? He shook his head in disbelief. He hadn't seen her in ten years and she just showed up at his parents' place? He was more confused by the moment.

Her blond waves spilled around her shoulders, just like when they were teens. Back when he'd thought they'd share their life together. But then, after high school graduation, she'd crushed him by ending communication between the two of them without ever discussing her reasons why. He had never even received a Dear John letter. To this day, he had questions. Evie squirmed and started fussing. He stood and crossed the room to create space between him and Brenna.

When she looked up, she met his mother's gaze and Brenna's shining eyes danced with joy. Boy, she was even more gorgeous than when they were in high school. Her baggy clothes hid her petite frame and were odd for her. His mother stood to hug his ex-girlfriend and Brenna's features lit with happiness.

Then her gaze landed on him and she stepped back in surprise. Her smile wavered and finally fell away as she focused on the ground. Her dog, some type of doodle with striking coloring, circled Brenna once and then sat beside her, leaning his snout on his owner's leg as though he was an emotional support dog. If so, why would she need one?

"Owen, this is my new co-leader for camp. You two are going to work so well together."

Cora's statement seemed to ring in the air around them. *You two are going to work so well together.* Brenna shot Owen a quick glance. He seemed as shocked as her.

The baby in his arms started squirming and making little noises of distress.

Why Owen? Though she knew he had returned to Serenity after the death of his wife, she hadn't expected to have to interact with him again.

"Cora," Brenna began, not sure where to start her questions. "What in the world do you mean? I thought you and I were going to run camp together." She crouched low to hug her dog, hating how shaky her voice sounded. She allowed Lulu to lean into her for comfort as she practiced the cleansing breaths her counselor had taught her. Maybe this wasn't panic she felt but shock at seeing him here. She wished she could return to the confident existence she'd enjoyed a year ago—a celebrated teacher enjoying life—not the fragile woman left in terror's wake.

The older lady nodded. "Let's move to the living room and get comfortable, shall we?" Brenna rose as Cora clumsily used her crutches to get to the next room.

Before Brenna could follow, Owen tugged at her arm and Lulu shifted between them, resting her snout on Brenna's thigh. Her gaze flickered to Cora hobbling away and then her devoted mini Bernedoodle.

"Last I heard," he started, "you had snagged a teaching position in a prestigious neighborhood near Dallas. What are you doing back here?" His nostrils flared as he waited for her answer. Well, she wasn't happy about their predicament either. She still couldn't quite believe she and her ex-boyfriend were in the same room together. When they'd parted ways after their high school graduation, she'd not expected to see him again. Especially because he now lived in North Carolina.

She lifted her chin and took a step away. Her counselor had taught her to always do what she could to be in control of difficult conversations. Well, if any conversation could be categorized as difficult, this was it.

"I moved back when your mother offered the

garage apartment during Christmas break," she said. About two weeks after she had survived the horrific home invasion, Cora had reached out to her about a camp detail and Brenna had spilled everything. When the older woman offered her the serene apartment for as long as she needed, Brenna had jumped at the chance.

"Sorry it isn't available for you and Evie to move into," she continued. His handsome features tightened at her apology and she felt guilty for being in the space. If she wasn't living in Cora's garage apartment, he and Evie would be able to set up home there. It would be perfect for him and the baby and they'd have much more privacy. She wanted to offer to move out, but she had no alternative housing options. Especially because she wasn't currently employed, though she hoped that would change sometime real soon.

"Not a problem. I wasn't expecting to return to Serenity." His shoulders dropped as though freshly remembering the reason he was here.

"I'm sorry about your wife." Since she didn't want to see the distress cross over his face, she dropped her gaze to Lulu.

"Listen, about co-leading—"

She put her hand up like a stop sign. "Let's see what your mother has to say, shall we?" Before he could answer, she turned and strode into the family room. She settled on the couch next to Cora, while Lulu sat at her feet. Brenna hadn't noticed the plethora of baby equipment in the room when she'd first arrived. The large space looked like a baby store had exploded in it.

"Mom, I'm going to get you a glass of water. I'll be right in," Owen called.

"I'm worried about him," Cora said in a soft voice. "I know we haven't always agreed with Owen's decisions." Her lips pursed and Brenna's mind went straight to the day when Owen's sister, Autumn, who was a dog trainer, had been teaching Brenna how to rely on Lulu for emotional support. Autumn had vented that her mother was still hurt by how Owen had treated their relationship over the years. Apparently, it was still strained. "But now that Willow is gone and he's become a single father, working at the camp will help him get back on his feet again."

"I understand." Brenna ran her hands along her cozy black sweatpants. Surely she and Cora could come to an understanding that would work for both of them. Cora rested her leg on top of the cushioned ottoman as a look of relief covered her face.

Owen returned, and placed the water glass next to his mother. Had he hit a growth spurt since high school? He seemed taller than the six-foot-one-inch teenager she'd dated. His brown hair had grown long and curled up at the back as though he needed a good trim. He'd always kept himself groomed nicely, but once he joined the military, he probably had a buzz cut. Now that he was out, maybe he was rebelling with a longer style. She couldn't help the small smile that lifted her lips. That seemed like something he would do.

He settled in a club chair across from her, attention on little Evie, a sappy and contented look on his face. The sweet sight brought tears to Brenna's eyes. She doubted she'd ever have a baby. Or a husband. Before the break-in and attack, she had no prospects and now, well, she couldn't imagine ever being at ease with a man again.

"I just can't run camp hobbling around on crutches," Cora stated, pulling Brenna's gaze from the captivating duo. "It's hard enough to do the basic things I need to throughout the day. I think I was a little too enthusiastic when I told you I could manage camp on crutches."

The words sank heavily in Brenna's gut, confirming Cora was serious about stepping away from the six-week camp. Her counselor had suggested that helping run camp would allow Brenna to move past the assault she'd endured last year and ease her toward a normal life. Since that night six months ago, she'd become insecure and unsure of herself, and she hated it. Cora must have noticed her furrowed brow because she took Brenna's hand.

"I know it isn't what we discussed. But I hadn't planned on falling and breaking my leg either. I'm sorry, but without Owen's help, I'm afraid we'll have to cancel camp this year."

Brenna swallowed the thick lump in her throat. The last thing she wanted was to disappoint Cora. The older woman had been so kind to her these past few months. And they couldn't cancel camp. Kids these days needed it as much as she had as a teen.

"No canceling, Mom. We can handle it," Owen stated firmly, shooting Brenna a look that seemed to say, *Work with me here. This will make my mother happy.* She rolled her eyes but gave him the slightest of nods. After all, she'd been childish in the way she'd ended things between them after graduation. She should at least try to get along with him.

"Oh, you two are simply the best," Cora stated as moisture collected in her eyes. "This takes a huge load off me." The older woman's smile trembled, filling Brenna with a sense of foreboding. Working with Owen was going to be awkward. Their history aside, she wasn't sure she was ready to trust any man. Even one she'd once thought she'd spend her life with.

Lulu, as though sensing the conflict and what it meant to her owner, flattened herself against Brenna's leg. She sank her fingers into her companion's tricolor fur and relished the immediate reassurance. Lulu had only been with her for two weeks, but had made a world of difference in reducing the number of agonizing panic attacks Brenna had and their length. She pressed a kiss against Lulu's white, black and chocolate forehead.

"The only thing you need to do is heal," Owen stated, then gave his mother a wink. He rose and placed the now-sleeping baby in a small bassinet between the two club chairs. He kept his focus on the little one long enough to show he was an attentive father.

There's nothing like a dreamy man with a precious child. His wife had probably been gorgeous, not someone who always wore black and baggy clothes to blend into the background like Brenna now did. Not someone forced to move away from her Dallas apartment because of constant panic attacks that rendered her unable to function. Though Brenna still experienced them here in Serenity, they weren't as frequent and severe. No, Owen's wife had likely been a confident and outgoing woman, the way Brenna had once been.

"Agreed," Brenna chimed in. "Whatever you

need, Cora." Though she wanted to ask the older woman to give them more details about splitting up responsibilities. Maybe they could divvy up the tasks and stay out of each other's way. With a baby to care for, that would probably work for him.

"Thank you. Both of you." Cora leaned forward, sticking her fingers into the cast to scratch. Given that camp was held in the humid outdoors—Cora would be even more miserable in the summer heat with that cast. With a look of relief on her face, Cora settled back against the couch.

Brenna laid a hand on her bouncing knee. This upsetting news made her downright fidgety. She moved her hand to her emotional support dog's head, taking comfort in her soft fur. The change of plans, and at such a late date, was just another thing for her to stress over.

Could the two of them come together and pull off an amazing camp experience for the children?

She wasn't sure, but they had to try because she'd made a commitment with Cora, and her counselor believed this step would help Brenna's healing process.

And the one thing Brenna wanted more than anything was to feel normal again.

Chapter Two

Two days later, Brenna tapped a closed marker to her chin and fretted over the list she'd written on the whiteboard. She glanced around the cramped camp office for escape routes—a door and a window. Of course, they could also be used for forced entry. Ever since the home invasion, she noticed these things. So, like her counselor recommended, she graded the space. She awarded this room a six out of ten for physical safety. But since she was on the Triple C Ranch property, there was an element of security, so she upped it to an eight, which was pretty good for her these days.

Lulu pressed her damp nose into Brenna's hand. Preoccupied with the list, she gave her dog a simple pat in response, finding her soft fur relaxing. While cows mooed in the distance, she eyed her watch. Five minutes late. How long could it take to walk over here from his parents' house a stone's throw away?

Right then, she heard footsteps—no, more like

boots clomping on cement flooring. She straightened her spine and hoped Owen would accept her list of divided responsibilities, because she didn't want to have to explain why she couldn't handle certain tasks. She felt powerless enough. She couldn't bear to have Owen see her weakness.

As he strode into the tiny office, the sight of his baby tucked into the blush pink front carrier against his chest took Brenna's breath away. She had to divert her gaze and compose herself. His wife probably purchased the baby carrier with no plans for Owen to use it, and now this sweet child was motherless. Brenna's heart cracked a little more because Owen had been through such a horrific tragedy and seemed to be handling the loss better than expected. Unlike how Brenna's past continued to haunt her every moment of every day.

"Hey, sorry I'm late." Owen rubbed the short hair on Evie's head as he focused on his baby. A silly grin splayed across his face, accentuating laugh lines around his eyes that she could barely see because of his tilted cowboy hat. Until now, Brenna hadn't realized how much she'd missed him.

"No worries." Why had Cora fallen? If she hadn't, the woman never would have asked Owen to co-lead the camp with Brenna. She could handle anyone but her ex-boyfriend, well, maybe. Regardless, after Brenna had walked away from Owen ten years ago, she didn't see how they could have a tolerable working relationship.

"Man, it's good to be back at the Triple C." He made cooing noises and she peeked at the duo. She couldn't help but smile. Owen was such an attentive father. Except he was gorgeous enough without adding an adorable baby to the mix.

"So, I thought you were a teacher," he stated, lifting his gaze from the baby and raising his eyebrows at her. "Are you going back to Dallas in the fall?" She narrowed her eyes at him. Was he trying to get rid of her?

"I'm not sure I want to teach anymore." The break-in had taken so much from her. Seemed baking was the only thing that calmed her and made her happy these days, but she couldn't make enough money to support herself with that expensive hobby. "In fact, I've decided to move back to Serenity. For good." She felt safe in her hometown and enjoyed the slower pace versus the rat race of Dallas. Now she needed to figure out a permanent place to live and get a job of some sort to provide for herself. But first things first—she needed to help run this summer camp. And succeed.

"What's going on?" He took a step closer and pointed at the whiteboard she'd been writing on all morning. She caught a whiff of soap from him and sweet baby shampoo from Evie. He nudged his Stetson back, the same worn cowboy hat he wore as a teen. His casual shorts and snug T-shirt were the opposite of her baggy pants and long-sleeve top. She tugged on her black shirt, snugging her hands into the soft fabric sleeves, finding comfort and safety in her oversize clothing.

"I thought I'd divvy up the responsibilities." She had decided to keep things strictly business and ignore their checkered past. "Camp starts on Monday, so we don't have much time." Butterflies fluttered in her belly in anticipation of the children arriving and learning and having fun. Part of her was excited, the other part nervous. Well, maybe petrified.

The kids didn't scare her, it was the unpredictable parents that worried her. Especially fathers or bossy mothers. She had never handled confrontation well. Now confrontations might send her into a downhill spiral.

Lulu leaned against Brenna again. Usually her mini Bernedoodle soothed her, but today the dog kept reminding Brenna how weak she had become since the forced entry and subsequent assault that had left her in the hospital for a week. The external injuries had healed, but the internal ones endured. Owen glanced at Lulu's distress but plowed forward.

"We are supposed to co-lead." His pinched expression showed he was clearly unhappy she'd taken on this responsibility on her own.

"We are, Owen. All I'm thinking about is the kids." If she didn't help him out, Cora would cancel camp. "You know how much this camp meant to me in high school."

"Put you on the straight and narrow," he said, his fingers shaping air quotes. Yes, she had probably said that phrase too much back when they'd started dating. But she'd been grateful for Cora and her team of volunteers.

"It also gave me hope for the future." And was the reason she'd selected teaching as a college major.

She took in the whiteboard and all the tasks she'd neatly written in columns. Her hope was that he'd be too overwhelmed with little Evie and just agree to her division of duties. She fisted her hands until her fingernails bit into her palms. Though she was willing to work hard, the possible parental interaction scared her. That was why his name was next to all the tasks that gave her stress to even consider.

"This probably isn't complete," she said, "but this is what I remember from last year." She waved at the whiteboard filled with dark blue *O*s next to his tasks and pink *B*s next to hers. Even though there were more *B*s than *O*s, his set chin had her worried.

He glimpsed out the window that framed a grouping of Angus cattle, grazing as though contemplating what to say. Indecision flitted over his face. When his gaze returned to her, it felt determined, maybe even tenacious. "Why did you block—"

"Not now, Owen," she said, a little more forcibly than she meant to. "Let's not talk about the past."

Brenna sank into the backless rolling chair and massaged her temples. Why had her and Owen's worlds collided at this precise moment?

"Okay. But we *will* talk about it." Then he pierced her with a look that dropped her focus to the cement floor. She wrapped her arms around herself, not at all looking forward to the future discussion.

A couple of weeks before their high school graduation, Owen had shared his dream with her—he planned to become a police officer. At eighteen, his announcement had rocked her world. Even though Owen eventually wanted a happily-ever-after with her, there was no way she could see herself with a police officer. Not after her father's injury in the line of duty had caused his paralysis from the waist down. His constant anger and verbal attacks against her and her mother had hurt.

No, she could never spend her life with someone who worked in a dangerous occupation for fear that he'd turn into her father. So when Owen had told her of his aspirations, she'd disappeared from his life without an explanation because she knew if she told him the truth, he might change his plans. And she didn't want to stand in the way of his dreams.

Frustrated by this fresh deluge of emotions, she twirled one of her fidget rings. As an eighteen-year-old, it had seemed like the easiest way to end things. Looking back, she had to admit she was being a coward. He deserved an apology today, but that would open the door to a conversation she wasn't prepared to have. She just wanted to ignore the past and focus her energy on recovering from the attack.

"Let's start over, shall we?" Owen took charge and grabbed the eraser, then swiped down the column that had their names marked in blue and pink. He placed the eraser back on the ledge and stepped back, looking pleased with himself.

Her eyes widened as her hard work disappeared. She gulped. There was no way she could handle interacting with people. Everything with Cora had been planned perfectly. They had agreed Cora would handle all the upset parents and volunteers and any men who showed up. And the two of them would work together to integrate Brenna's forward-thinking ideas into the six-week camp. Now Owen.

"Co-leaders, right?" He plucked the red pen, uncapped it and wrote her name next to the first item—lead morning drop-off. Brenna inhaled sharply right as something startled Evie and got the baby crying. Owen wrapped his arms around the baby and started bouncing to calm her.

With him distracted by Evie's fussing, Brenna tried to get a handle on what was happening. Lead drop-off meant she'd be in charge of any issues that came up when the children arrived in the morning. Any parent who had questions or concerns would come to her. And Brenna knew she couldn't handle it. Because there were always problems. And it was the problems that inevitably led to confrontation, which Brenna feared the most. But she couldn't admit her weakness to Owen. Not after she'd hurt him the way she had.

Before she could think more about it, she used her index finger to wipe away her name. For the moment, the empty whiteboard space gave her relief.

"I'd rather not be responsible for that one," she said, hoping her voice didn't sound as tight to him as it did to her. His bouncing seemed to appease the baby as she'd quieted down.

He frowned. "How about I handle camp on my own, then? I don't see how this has turned into a two-person job."

At his announcement, she sucked in a surprised breath and contemplated an escape to her apartment to bake a few dozen cookies. That would ground her, make her feel better. But no, running wasn't an option. She had to be stronger, push herself, stand up to him.

"No, Owen. Your mother asked us to co-lead." She straightened, longing for the confidence she'd had before her world had turned upside down.

If she'd learned nothing else these past few months, it was that she had to stand up for herself, because no one else would.

This woman was driving Owen bonkers. "My mother has worked camp solo for years. I can do the same."

"She may have handled things on her own in the past, but she asked us to co-lead. And co-lead we will," Brenna stated firmly as she stepped up to the whiteboard and uncapped a black marker while staring at the list she'd written earlier. Though she sounded confident, her hand shook.

He swiped at his tired and scratchy eyes. Unfortunately, she had a point. His mother had asked him to co-lead. And he didn't want to disappoint her, not when she was giving him a chance at redemption. He plucked a marker off the ledge. Brenna promptly moved away, Lulu remaining at her side. Might as well knock this list out. The quicker they divided the responsibilities, the quicker he could get out of here.

"Lead morning drop-off," he read the first thing on her list. Why was she so opposed to this task? He remembered her as being outgoing. Though her entire personality seemed a bit out of whack right now for some reason.

"If you could do that, I'd appreciate it," she chimed in. He stared at the board and absently rubbed Evie's back with circle strokes. What was her issue with being the lead for drop-off? His frustration built. "Is it because you've been gone from Serenity for a while and you think it'll be uncomfortable?" He guessed.

"That's one reason," she said from her seat on the rolling chair. The dog placed her chin on Brenna's lap.

He shrugged, confident there was more to it, but she clearly had no intention of revealing why, so he wrote his name next to the task. It made sense for a McCaw to be the front person for it, anyway. They worked through a couple more items. Clearly Brenna was willing to work, but for some reason the drop-off thing bothered her.

"Evie has a hard time going down for her last nap of the day, which coincides with the afternoon drop-off. Can you do that one?" He wrote her name next to that piece.

"How about I handle it on Monday, then we can talk about it?" At her response, he raked a hand through his hair. He couldn't figure her out. Did she want to help or not? "Oh, don't forget about the Saturday morning volunteer meeting." Her voice sounded confident, contradicting how she appeared. He wasn't sure how to deal with her alternating attitude. She was uncooperative one minute and helpful the next.

"Sorry, but I can't make it. I promised to work cattle with my father on Saturday." He made his way to the door.

"Wait." Brenna's voice wavered. What was going on with her these days?

Baffled at her command, he turned and noted Lulu was glued to her side. Even upset, Brenna was still as pretty as he remembered. Maybe even more.

She schooled her face and that tenacity he recalled from high school flashed across her features.

"Listen, I work at the bakery every Saturday morning, but I cut my hours short to be at the scheduled meeting. Anyway, I need you to attend. Your mother asked us to co-lead, remember?" A clear message to his reference of handling camp on his own.

She had a point. Since he was trying to mend his relationship with his parents, maybe insisting on doing camp alone wouldn't go over well. His mother seemed bent on including Brenna for some reason.

Except, he wasn't sure he could work with Brenna.

Evie stirred as he mulled over the woman in front of him. After high school, she had blocked his number and left town for the summer, confusing him to no end and breaking his heart in the process. Even after all that, he couldn't deny he still cared for Brenna. She'd been his first love, so he'd never forget her. Except her past actions taught him that love hurt.

If they were going to work together, he'd need some answers. He looked at Brenna and waited until she gazed up at him. It was brief, but eye contact just the same.

"Why did you block my phone number after graduation?"

Her eyes widened and something like wariness scurried across her face. Whatever the emotion, it wasn't good. It made all his prior questions resurface.

Before he could push her, Evie startled and began crying again. She sounded like a lawn mower starting all slow like and then revving up high. Her cries turned into wails, so he unbuckled her from the carrier and checked her diaper. Dry. He put his clean index finger into her mouth, like his mother had taught him, and she didn't suck like she was hungry. She shouldn't be, as she had downed a full bottle before he'd come over, which was why he had been a few minutes late.

Gently, he bounced her on his shoulder, then on his chest, just like he'd seen his mother do, but to no avail.

Brenna moved closer to him. The closest she'd been since they reconnected. He could smell the faint rose fragrance in her shampoo, the same kind she'd used in high school. Her focus was on Evie, not him. Just like the other day, she was wearing black baggy clothing, as though she wanted to disappear into the background.

Instead of the outgoing and carefree person he remembered from high school, she seemed more cautious. Maybe even scared of the world.

She put her palm on Evie's head and touched her. Something akin to awe settled on his ex-girlfriend's features. Lulu pressed herself against Brenna's leg. She patted her gorgeous multicolor dog with her other hand but didn't take her eyes off Evie.

"Can I hold her?" Brenna asked. He could barely hear her over his baby's howling.

"Have at it," he said.

She leaned in and lifted Evie into her arms. He took a step away, still confused and hurt that she had ghosted him ten years ago, but after her agitated reaction a few minutes ago, he wasn't going to press for answers. Now wasn't the time.

Though he still cared for her and wanted the best for her, he didn't really want her in his life. Not without an explanation. Because she had crushed him.

Evie had settled down with a little jostling and soft cooing. His heart melted at seeing his baby transformed from upset to joyful so quickly. How had Brenna done that? His mother had the "baby touch" as well. He only seemed to have the knack of making Evie happy in the middle of the night.

He scrubbed a hand over his face. Owen felt like he was failing at being a father.

A sudden, shy smile blossomed over Brenna's face as she swayed back and forth with Evie and gazed at her. Her relaxed stance was the opposite of her new uptight attitude. A lock of her blond hair fell in front of her face, covering his view.

Right then, he realized the reason she had

blocked his number probably didn't matter. It was in the past.

Anyway, he had found Willow. Married her. He thought his heart had been restored. And now, with the accident, his heart was shattered once again. He knew he was strong, but one could only handle so much. Now he was focused solely on Evie—where his attention would stay.

He tipped the brim of his old Stetson back. Thanks to the intense heat, sweat clung to the inner band. Earlier, he'd had to dust the thing off before he put it on. It amazed him how easily he'd fallen back into the habits he had as a teenager growing up on the Triple C Ranch. He sure hoped he wouldn't pick up the habit of taking a liking to Brenna as he had as a teen. Though that shouldn't be hard, since his long-held resentment about the way she'd abruptly cut off contact with him ran deep. Anyway, he never planned on falling in love again.

"She's adorable," Brenna said, keeping her focus on the baby. "Oh, good news. I've secured six morning and four afternoon mothers who jumped at the opportunity to volunteer for a reduced camper rate."

"What?" His body tensed at her out-of-context announcement. He knew the full camper fee allowed his mother to run the camp at no cost. That was one thing she prided herself on. Discounted rates meant money would have to come out of his mother's pocket to cover the expenses.

"It's a good deal because there weren't enough volunteers last year."

He flattened his lips together to stop from saying something he might regret. At the moment, he felt like a fuse about to explode because Brenna didn't understand how the finances worked. Wait until his mother heard about this.

He needed to leave, so he snagged Evie, stepped around Brenna and out of the coffin-like office. He rushed across the gravel and stomped up his parents' front steps.

His mother sat on the couch, her injured leg elevated on the coffee table, a pillow underneath. But before he could utter a word, his mother spoke.

"Did you and Brenna just meet?"

"Yes, I—"

"I'm sorry I dozed off earlier and didn't hear you leave," she interrupted him. "I neglected to tell you that a while back, Brenna and I split up the responsibilities. Basically, anything dealing with parents or male volunteers, I promised I would handle. So I'd like you to honor that."

"Okay," he said. "Why?"

"Something happened which brought her back to Serenity," she said. "But it isn't my story to share."

He settled his now-sleeping Evic in the bassinet, replaying Brenna's actions and hesitations through his mind. The dog. Her insecurities. Caring for Evie must have muddled his police-trained brain for him to miss the obvious clues. Now he felt bad about erasing those *B*s and *O*s off the whiteboard and acting like he didn't want her help. He should probably be more compassionate. She was certainly being compassionate toward him about the loss of his wife.

Then he recalled the reason he'd rushed over. He informed his mother about Brenna's outlandish offer to parents who were willing to volunteer. "Mom, you'll operate with a loss for the year or, worse yet, it'll run the camp into the ground."

She frowned at him. "First off, Owen, God is in control. If He wants this camp to continue, it will. Second, the camp is in existence for once reason: to share the Good News with those who need it. Third, Brenna has a spark about her and great ideas." She took a sip of the water next to her, then leaned back. "You are right, the cost from each camper allows me to run camp in the black, but Brenna also came up with the idea of getting businesses to donate products instead of me paying full price. She's been working for two months to bring her ideas to fruition. So no, Owen, those ten reduced camper rates won't impact my bottom line. Instead, with Brenna's hard work, camp is actually running in the black with a little slush fund for next year."

"But Mom, what you've done for the past twenty-five years has worked. Why change it?" Even though he hadn't been back to visit, he'd kept up with the family news over the years. His brothers would have told him if his mother had made any camp changes. And they hadn't mentioned a thing.

"Because Brenna has great ideas. Just because it has been working doesn't mean I was being as effective as possible. Owen, I've had a year to pray over this and the Lord has impressed upon me to embrace Brenna and her innovative ideas. Just because you are a McCaw doesn't mean you know what's best for our family-run camp." She withdrew her fingers from the cast and leaned back, clearly not only frustrated with her itchy broken leg but with him as well.

He gulped down a retort because he felt like he was on thin ice with his family. And if he was smart, he'd keep his thoughts to himself. Especially thoughts about Brenna, who seemed to have won over his mom big-time.

Since his mother seemed to be counting on Brenna, he sure hoped she wouldn't abandon his mom like she had dumped him all those years ago.

Chapter Three

On the outskirts of the Triple C Ranch, Owen adjusted his sweaty Stetson while working the cattle with his family. It felt good to be back atop his childhood horse, with the symphony of singing birds, cows mooing and the creak of the saddle leather as Cinnamon strode along.

He'd done this countless times—could do it blindfolded—but today felt different. He and his brother Ethan were wrangling the remaining herd from the rear. Their father was up ahead, riding back and forth, pushing the teeming livestock closer to the first crowding area. Bandit, the ranch's golden retriever, was his father's partner. Over the years, the dog had learned to herd just like a border collie, making him indispensable on days like today.

Owen pressed his heels into the chestnut horse beneath him and steered to the left and then back to the right to direct the cattle. The movement of the cows' hooves created a swirling dust that had become heavier as the day wore on.

"Thanks for being here today," Ethan said as their paths met. They both kept their focus on the cattle and the goal of moving them forward. Owen took a deep breath, reveling in the familiar smells of cattle, horses and ranch air. He hadn't realized how much he'd missed living in the country.

"Happy to help." Even though cattle ranching wasn't Owen's dream, he had hoped to work the cattle with his father while he figured out what the future held for him. In an attempt to cool down, he plucked the collar of his long-sleeve chambray work shirt and flapped it against his damp torso, but it didn't help.

"Still adjusting to working in the outdoors, I see." Ethan smirked. "You'll get used to it right quick." Even though, as a police officer, Owen was sometimes outdoors when he worked, he was always able to slip in and out of the patrol car or precinct air conditioning.

He took in the cattle and the wide-open pastures and wondered if he could join Ethan and his father at the ranch. His brother Walker managed a horse farm up the road and his baby brother Carter was an accountant, so Ethan was the only family member helping his dad. If Owen wasn't returning to law enforcement, joining them would be a distinct possibility. Ranching would be the easy answer. And it was a safe profession. He could build on the plot of land his parents had reserved for him. Wouldn't have a commute. He'd have built-in babysitters to help him out. Somewhat flexible hours. He fussed with Cinnamon's mane, dreading having to make a decision. This could work, but did he want to be a cattle rancher?

"Dad's thrilled to have you here," Ethan stated, his hand resting on his worn saddle horn as he came to a stop because of the bottleneck up ahead.

Owen glanced at his father, whose cowboy hat shaded his leathered face. His grin did appear more sparkling than normal. His expression could mean he was happy to have Owen here, or maybe it was simply from working the cattle. His father liked to get eyes on the herd. And vaccination days were one of the few times he saw them all in a day.

"Maybe." As Owen shifted in his saddle, a grumbling noise sounded to his right. A small group of cows had gotten out of line and lumbered toward a clump of grass that was somehow alive in all this tamped-down dirt. Owen looped back to corral them with the others, then removed his Stetson and swiped sweat off his brow, eyeing his father on horseback.

"I'm happy he reached out for help today," he told his brother. "Seems like he's treating me like normal." Or like a loving father treated his children. The distance between him and his parents was all his fault. He saw that now.

"I get the impression Dad is happy to have you back," Ethan stated, "but it'll take Mom a little bit of time. She's more hurt than he is. Seems like he has a shorter memory."

Owen's chest panged with the years he'd had limited contact with his parents. He'd been selfish. Thankfully, Willow had worked at establishing a relationship with his parents, especially his mother. He'd always be grateful for her persistence and his parents' gracious attitude toward her, even when he was being a jerk.

"When Willow became pregnant, we both realized how much we missed the McCaw family and how we wanted you all to be a big part of our baby's life." He switched the reins to his other hand. "Since Willow was an only child, she wanted our baby to grow up knowing her cousins and aunts and uncles and both sets of grandparents." His chest ached recalling that conversation. "But I hadn't gotten around to reconciling with Mom and Dad." Now he wished he could have a do-over, but that wasn't possible.

"Mom would love to hear that. She adored Willow."

The lump in Owen's throat grew. He didn't

want to talk about the strained relationship with his parents anymore.

"So I'm thinking I might retire from law enforcement."

Ethan eyed him. "Seriously?"

"Yep."

"Police work has always been your dream. What gives?"

"Now that I'm a single dad, it's probably not the safest profession." Oddly, saying this out loud didn't dredge up regret. In fact, he felt pretty calm and collected about his decision. Ethan nodded, looking grim. If he wasn't going to be a police officer anymore, Owen needed to figure out what his new career would be. He had to provide for his daughter. And get out of his parents' house. If Brenna wasn't staying in the garage apartment, he could move in there and have a little more privacy. But he couldn't change the situation, so he pushed away his resentment toward her living conditions.

"Any thought about what you might do?"

"None. Back in North Carolina, I volunteered with the youth at our church and loved it. But volunteering to help teens won't bring in a paycheck. And I need to support Evie."

They moved the cattle along and Ethan caught him up on what had been happening with his three children, making Owen regret all the times he could have returned for special events but hadn't. He missed being with family and enjoyed the back-and-forth with his brother. There was something comfortable and personal about being here.

As the day progressed, he remembered why he hadn't wanted to stay in Serenity and become a rancher with his dad. Working cattle didn't excite him like the adventure that came with each fresh shift of police work. A painful lump sat in his throat at the realization.

Owen would help for the remainder of the day, but he needed to figure out what to do with his life if not ranching. And preferably before camp ended so he could get a new career started. He glanced ahead at his father. Hopefully he wouldn't be too disappointed that Owen decided against ranching. Again.

In his peripheral vision, movement caught his eye. One of the ranch's utility terrain vehicles was approaching them at a very slow clip. Who was driving the vehicle in such a tentative manner?

As it got closer, he spotted Brenna behind the wheel, with Lulu beside her panting. Today, her hair was pulled back in a ponytail, wisps flowing freely in the breeze. Worry lined her features. But the moment their eyes met, relief replaced the worry, and she pointed the UTV in his direction.

Even though he was still upset she had blocked his number after graduation, he was saddened she wasn't the chipper and confident person he'd known. Her changed personality gave him a hankering to protect her, which irked him. He was mad at her and she didn't deserve his kindness. He blew out a frustrated breath and trotted to the fence near where she was parking, while trying to ignore how his legs were screaming at him because they weren't used to being in a saddle.

She parked and lifted a cell phone. His eyes widened as the empty spot in his back pocket lay flat against the saddle instead of feeling the bulk of a phone. When he reached the fence, his horse shook his head, his mane flowing with the movement. Brenna gave the chestnut a small smile and rubbed a hand along the bridge of Cinnamon's nose.

"Your mom found this in the diaper bag and thought you might need it," she said, her gaze on the horse. A flicker of something crossed over her tense face. Panic? He wasn't sure, but before he could place it, she pushed a loose tendril of hair away from her chin. Did she remember when she had helped work the cattle back in high school? They had been on foot in charge of one of the crowding areas all day. He'd loved spending a chunk of time with her, conversing about everything under the sun. Now was different. He wasn't thrilled to be pushed together with her.

He reached for the phone, his link to his mother in case Evie needed him. "Thanks." He slid the device securely into his back pocket, feeling bad about rushing away from Brenna yesterday. But when she brought up the subject of reduced camper rates for volunteering parents, he'd gotten irritated. Once his mother had explained everything, he realized he might have overreacted, though he still didn't understand why things around the camp needed to change. Before he could broach the topic to apologize, she spoke.

"I got the text message you sent to the volunteers last night," she said. Her chin was lifted like she was ready for a fight.

"Good. Glad I got your number right." He gave her a smile, wondering where she was going with this.

Her lips parted, then she clamped her mouth shut, lips drawn in a narrow line, and frowned. "No, Owen, you moved the volunteer meeting without talking with me about it." She stuck her hands on her hips, but even with the baggy clothing he could tell she was still slender. "What if I wasn't available on Sunday evening?"

"Then I'd handle it without you." He shrugged.

She'd told him she didn't want to be in charge of the meeting alone. What choice did he have?

"No. We're in this together." She pierced him with a look that made him wonder if he should have consulted her. No. He didn't have to run every little decision past her. "You don't get to make unilateral decisions," she stated with a determination he hadn't seen in her since high school. Before he could respond, she walked away.

He sat there, dumbfounded. Maybe something had happened in her past to make her cautious around strangers. But her confidence seemed to be quickly returning. At least around him.

He joined Ethan, slowly moving the cattle to their destination.

"How is it, ya know, working with Brenna?" his brother asked.

"I'm just helping Mom with camp." Cinnamon tossed his head to get rid of the hovering flies.

"Think you guys will get back together?" Owen bristled that his brother would think he could move on from Willow so quickly.

"Trust me when I say we will never get back together." Brenna had hurt him. He would not allow that to happen again. His jaw tightened with determination.

Ethan shifted his cowboy hat and said nothing, which made Owen want to defend himself even more. But he kept his mouth shut, zigzagging behind the cattle.

That brief mention of camp reminded him to connect with his siblings, maybe even his sisters-in-law, to make sure his mother would be able to babysit Evie even with a broken leg. He took the opportunity to explain the situation to his brother, who readily agreed to organize everyone and make sure their mother would have the necessary support while she was caring for Evie. Owen's chest filled with gratitude to be back home. To have a family that cared for and nurtured their own.

Yes, he craved to fix the rift with his parents and hoped effectively handling camp for his mother would be a large start, if not the key for repairing the divide. But he hadn't realized how much he, and Willow, had missed by not returning to Texas to visit. He'd fallen back into a satisfying rapport with his siblings, and his new brother-in-law and sisters-in-law had readily accepted him, and for that he was grateful. Now to work on his parents.

Before long, they were close to having all the cattle enclosed in the crowding areas and their father joined them, herding the final few.

His father neared and then slapped Owen on the shoulder. "I never thought I'd see my city boy

back on horseback at the Triple C ever again."
His weathered face grinned up at him.

Owen shifted in his saddle and averted his
gaze in case his father could tell what he was
thinking. Yes, he was back at the Triple C because his life had taken an unexpected turn and
he needed somewhere safe and familiar to figure out his next steps. But ranching full-time?
No way.

He stole a glance at his father, whose features
were laced with eagerness. Now was not the time
to voice his decision.

He didn't want to hurt his father's feelings
nor damage his chance to mend the relationship
with his parents.

The day of stress baking hadn't helped. Brenna
lifted the cake-like cookie and swiped vanilla
frosting on one side, chocolate on the other. Her
exasperation over Owen's reaction to the parent
volunteers yesterday was at an all-time high.

She blew a strand of hair away from her face
and started another cookie. She had no idea
what had set him off, but when she mentioned
the handful of reduced camper rates, he had
clammed up and stomped away like a child. He
acted as if he believed she was doing something
underhanded to his mother. She would never. He
should know her better than that.

She slapped the spatula full of icing on the cookie, splattering the sugary goo on the counter. Lulu scrambled over from her spot in the sun to investigate. She must have found some icing, because she licked the floor in a number of locations and then sat at attention, eyeing Brenna's hands.

Being around Owen was hard and annoying, but oddly, she felt like herself around him. More confident. More like she could assert her wishes. Kind of like how she'd let him know her thoughts earlier when she'd delivered his phone. She smiled. That had felt good. Maybe a step closer to being back to her normal self.

She finished frosting the cookie in her hand, feeling unsettled. She glanced at the time—way too early for Owen to be back from helping his father with the cattle. Maybe a visit with Cora would perk her up. After she plated some black-and-white cookies, the ones she'd frosted earlier, and washed her hands, she walked over to the big house to gather some confidence from Cora, Lulu trailing behind. She knocked on the front door and let herself in.

Earlier, when Cora had asked her to take Owen's cell phone to him, all Brenna could think about were those fun high school weekends when she'd joined him and his family to work the cattle. At that time, the dysfunction in her house was at an all-time high, so spending time with the McCaws was a blessing. Not to mention working side by side with Owen had been wonderful.

But now was a different story. Owen was upset with her about how she'd ended things between them after high school and she couldn't handle dredging up the past. Their spending time together simply wasn't wise.

"Those look yummy, Brenna. What are they?" Cora's gaze never left the plate of cookies, even when Brenna set them on the coffee table.

"Half-moon cookies. I had them years ago when we visited Upstate New York and just had to give myself a shot at recreating them." Lulu tagged behind as she peeked into the bassinet where Evie lay sleeping.

Cora selected one of the cookies that had a dense cake base and thick frosting. She bit into the cookie, leaned back and moaned as she chewed. "This is amazing. Tastes like something from a high-end bakery."

Brenna grinned and settled in a cozy chair, pulling her knees up to her chest. "Thank you. I've found baking comforting these past six months." And Mabel, the owner of Mabel's Diner, had asked if she'd be willing to supply two dozen every Saturday morning on her way to the bakery. Brenna had accepted the opportunity and was excited with the amount of money she'd be making.

"I'm glad to hear that. Have you ever thought about turning baking into a career?"

"A career? No." Brenna chuckled. "I don't think I could make a living from baking." Though that would be nice. Sure, she loved her Saturday mornings at the bakery, but there was an element of stress when she was there. Baking in her kitchen was much more relaxing. And this opportunity with Mabel was an enjoyable addition to her ho-hum life, but nothing that would pay the bills. She just might have to return to teaching. But first things first, she needed to get through camp and gain her confidence back.

"I think you could swing it." Cora put the remainder of the cookie on a napkin and set it on the table beside her right as Evie let out a cry, which started low and motored up to a screech pretty quickly. Before Brenna could stand to help, Cora gathered the baby in her arms and plucked a bottle from the bottle warmer beside her. Once her needs were met, Evie quieted.

Cute sucking noises came from the baby and Brenna couldn't take her eyes off the sweet bundle in Cora's arms.

"Would you like to finish feeding her?" Cora asked. Brenna's heart flip-flopped with the thought of holding that little cutie-pie again. She forced herself not to jump right up. Instead she took her time moving over to Cora and slipping her hands under Evie's warm little body.

Evie seemed disturbed at the change in hands, but soon snuggled into the crook of Brenna's arm. She smelled clean and precious, like all babies. But for some reason, Evie seemed special, for she had captured Brenna's heart from their first meeting.

Brenna settled in her chair, with Lulu sitting at her feet as though not only guarding her but the baby as well. She relaxed against the soft cushion. She could sit here holding Evie and staring at her all day. Hopefully, Cora didn't mind the break in the conversation.

With her index finger, she lightly traced Evie's face from her hairline to her chin. The baby stopped sucking her bottle and stared at Brenna. Could a child this young focus? Brenna wasn't sure, but she made silly faces, trying to get her to smile anyway. She didn't know much about children. But somehow Evie had wormed her way into her heart, which was fine because the baby no longer had a mother and deserved to be treasured.

What would it be like to be a mother?

After the break-in and attack, she couldn't imagine herself ever being able to trust a man enough to marry him. She pushed the morose thoughts away and aimed her attention at the adorable child in her arms.

"You are so pretty," Brenna whispered. Evie stopped sucking the bottle and her brows scrunched together as though in worry. Brenna almost rushed her back to Cora, but as quick as the baby stopped, she started eating again, now staring up at the slow-moving ceiling fan overhead.

"Brenna, what a pleasant surprise," Wade McCaw startled her out of her baby trance. He laid his hand on her shoulder and squeezed. She looked up at him and smiled, hoping the embarrassment of being consumed with little Evie didn't show on her face. His fatherly grin warmed her core.

She'd been living in the garage apartment for nearly six months. In that time, Cora and Wade had made her feel like family. Not an afterthought like her parents, but supported and loved. And after Cora heard about the assault, she hadn't judged her at all. Her parents would judge. They'd find her at fault for not having a more secure apartment. Even though her parents still lived in Serenity, she had yet to stop by. Their constant bickering would drain her precarious energy. And she couldn't afford that. Not with camp starting Monday. Though she knew she had to face them. Her counselor had urged her to confront her home situation so she'd find peace with her parents.

She tipped her head against his hand, thankful for this couple and their stabilizing personalities. They'd stepped into her life when she needed them. If it wasn't for the McCaws and their sweet nature, she wouldn't have any confidence around people. But Owen's parents had treated her with love, as they always had, and their kindness had helped her see that people she already knew weren't scary. It was only strangers that made her uneasy.

"Cookies!" Wade exclaimed as he moved to the coffee table and nabbed what might have been the biggest one on the plate. He bit into it and moaned, exclaiming how good it was. "Boys, cookies in here."

Her eyes widened. Sure enough, Owen and his brother skidded into the room, jabbing at each other like they were teenagers again. Owen's chocolate eyes twinkled with merriment. He ran a hand over his sweaty, light brown locks, making several sections stand on end. The motion highlighted his broad, muscular chest covered with a long-sleeve chambray work shirt.

She averted her gaze, wanting to be anywhere but here. Because if she were honest with herself, she'd never gotten over him. Even though he had married and, from what she'd heard, was happy, there was a wound that had never fully healed—at least on her end. Except she wasn't sure she could ever reveal why she'd walked away from their promising relationship. Now that years had passed, the reason seemed selfish, almost immature. But at the time, her reasoning had felt solid.

Cora wrestled with her crutches, then stood and placed them under her arms and headed down the hallway.

Meanwhile, Owen and Ethan each grabbed a cookie. When Owen turned around, he spotted her and his head jerked back as though surprised to find her there. Probably because of how she had stomped away from him in the open field this morning. But she couldn't help it. He irritated her.

"We still haven't finished splitting responsibilities," he said. But she needed to clear the air between them first. Brenna paused and while the baby kept slurping up her bottle, she gathered the courage to speak.

"You know, you made me uncomfortable when the whole parents with reduced camper rates came up." For some reason, she had her confidence back around him. And for that, she was grateful. "You do understand we're fifty-fifty running the camp, right?" Before he could answer, she noticed Wade and Ethan raise their brows and bolt to the safety of the kitchen with their cookies. Her tone may have been a little sharp, but it didn't seem like Owen respected her position as co-leader.

"Sorry I rushed out yesterday," he said. "My mother explained everything to me. Well, not everything. Just what you and she had agreed to." But the way his lips scrunched up, she wondered if he agreed to the plans she and Cora had for camp. Or was he just playing nice? "I understand how my mother wants the camp run. She wants Victory Youth Camp to be a rousing success this year. And I, for one, plan to make that happen."

"Same here." He took Evie from her arms and they divided up the rest of the responsibilities. Thankfully, he took everything dealing with parents, which relieved Brenna to no end. Things were looking good for camp on Monday.

"I still need you to handle afternoon drop-off since it conflicts with Evie's last nap of the day."

Her heart raced. She had assumed from the talk he had with his mother that he understood her reticence to deal with parents. From her days of teaching a variety of grades, she knew parents of older kids had less patience. If she could pick morning or afternoon parents to deal with, she'd pick morning any day of the week. Anyway, Cora could handle putting the baby down for her nap, so what was his problem?

Realization hit her in the gut. Maybe the only way out of this mess was to tell him about the home invasion.

Lulu firmly laid her furry snout in Brenna's lap and gave her a reassuring look. Brenna focused on the calming brown orbs among all the errant hair sticking up in the dog's face and considered her options.

She had hoped to get away with co-leading and not telling him about her past. But he was making her play her hand, and she didn't like it one bit.

Chapter Four

Monday morning, Brenna and Owen and the volunteers huddled in the shade of the pavilion, prepared for the campers to arrive. Everyone appeared excited for the first day of camp as they awaited the arrival of the first car or minivan and chatted among themselves.

Except Brenna. Her stomach roiled with nervousness. Ever since the forced entry, whenever she got nervous, all she wanted to do was curl up in a ball and lie on the couch. Or her bed. Anywhere she was alone.

She shook away the yearning and pulled her hands into her overly long sleeves. Lulu noticed her agitation and leaned against Brenna. Thankful for her dog, she petted Lulu, who sported her red vest today so campers would know she was working.

Under the brim of his cowboy hat, Owen captured her gaze and smiled. His brown hair curled out from beneath the back of his Stetson and his eyes were kind, as though he was okay being her co-leader. She hoped he'd prove that by keeping his word. He strode toward her.

She glanced at Cora's house, just a stone's throw away, and wished her friend were here with her. But instead, she had Owen.

"You okay? You're kind of pale," Owen stated. Concern lined his features.

No. She wasn't all right. Not at all. Her insides were tangled in knots. She tightened her grip on the edges of her sleeves and forced a smile, shuddering at how twisted her face must look. Maybe she should have taken him aside over the weekend and informed him about the break-in and the reason she had Lulu. But she had chickened out.

"I'm good." She searched for something neutral to discuss in an attempt to take her mind off the upcoming deluge of parents with questions. "Why was the camp pavilion built so close to your parents' house?"

"They never imagined the camp would grow this large." He chuckled. "Twenty-five years ago my mother didn't think her tiny seed of an idea would flourish like this." She nodded. Still nervous, but having him nearby helped.

The sun was still low in the clear blue sky, but it was already warm. What else should she expect for June in northern Texas?

"Afternoon camp is going to be downright

hot," she said. See, she could have a conversation while stressing over the upcoming day.

"Well, then, I'm glad someone planned water games for the kids today." He gave her an appreciative smile, referring to the details they'd hashed out after the volunteer meeting last night. She hadn't remembered how scatterbrained he could be. Thankfully, she had tons of ideas in her head from years of teaching.

A gray minivan pulled in and her breath snagged in her throat. The tires crunched over gravel, growing louder as the vehicle neared, making her heart race. She took a step back, trying to hide in the shadows.

She could do this, right? She had Owen and a bevy of sweet volunteers to back her up. Except none of them knew about her fears. Maybe she'd made a mistake by not telling them.

Harriet, one of their morning-only volunteers, walked over. "Brenna, the baked goods you made were delicious. Thank you. And the variety. You must have been up all night."

Thankful for the distraction, she took in the older lady's face, crinkled in just the right places. Harriet was someone she'd known for almost her whole life. "You are welcome. I'm glad you enjoyed them." Harriet moved back to her position as a car door slammed. Brenna hadn't been able to sleep last night, so she did the only thing that calmed her—baking. The volunteers had received the fruit of her middle-of-the-night labors.

She shifted her attention to the parking area that the Triple C Ranch horse barn shared with the camp, surprised to see so many cars and minivans and extended cab pickup trucks amid the kicked-up gravel dust. Her heart skipped a beat. She hadn't expected everyone to arrive at once. Doors slammed and parents walked to the pavilion while children raced over.

"Do you hear that?" Owen asked, his eyebrows scrunched together in worry. "Evie is crying." He turned and rushed to his mother's house, the large green door gulping him up. Her eyes widened at his abrupt departure. What was going on?

Brenna rubbed her sweaty hands down the length of her oversize, nylon hiking pants, hating the thin fabric, but she figured it would keep her cooler on this summer day. She and Owen had planned for him to be in charge of drop-off and pickup. Had he forgotten?

"Brenna? I'm Lauren Humphries, Olivia's mother." The woman's hand rested on a little girl who must have been about six years old, while her other hand clutched an admission form. "Olivia has a nut allergy." She proceeded to tell Brenna that she'd filled in the information on the paper form and emailed Cora, but wanted to make doubly sure everyone knew about the allergy.

This was an easy one. Having been a third-grade teacher, Brenna knew how to handle anxious parents. She soothed the mother's concerns and wiped the worry off her face. Lauren walked her daughter to the designated drop-off area, pushing the form into Harriet's hands and likely reminding her about the allergy as well.

Brenna got it. Parents couldn't get complacent with their children's safety.

She released a relieved breath that she'd been able to push her fears away and deal with a worried mother. Hopefully, that was the only issue to arise with Owen gone.

She swung her gaze around. While she'd been speaking with Lauren, a line had collected with other parents. A knot formed in her belly. Where was Owen? And who in the world had passed the word that Brenna was in charge? Man, she missed Cora. Cora could handle each parent with the love and finesse necessary. But Cora wasn't here.

By the fourth parent question, sweat dripped down Brenna's back along her spine. It was either from her cozy long-sleeved top making her too warm, or nerves. At this point, she couldn't tell, but she guessed it was from the heat.

"You should wear short sleeves, Brenna. You're going to be too hot in that outfit," one mother said, as though Brenna hadn't considered and rejected that idea on numerous occasions. Even lost sleep weighing the pros and cons of lighter clothing to stay cooler versus her usual attire that comforted her. At least she'd purchased these breathable hiking pants. Except the fabric draping along her legs, even though an airy material, still had some warmth to it. But it didn't have the comfort of her cotton sweatpants. However, the long sleeves and pants didn't seem to have made her disappear into the background like she'd hoped—apparently, the parents believed she was in charge.

As that mother made her way to the pavilion with her little one, Esther, their lead volunteer, stopped by to thank her for the cookies and muffins. "You should sell your baked goods," she told her. As if. Sure, Mabel paid her to deliver half-moon cookies once a week, but she'd need a lot more Mabels to make baking more than a hobby. Not that she wanted to push herself into starting a business, because that sounded scary and completely out of reach. Anyway, baking was an expensive hobby, not a way to make a living.

Brenna gave the volunteer a courteous smile and nod, and then listened to the concerns of the next parent in line. If she could just get through the morning drop-off, she'd survive. At least, she hoped this would be the hardest part. Frustration at Owen's sudden disappearance built. She had wondered if putting her guard up around him was the fair thing to do. But this morning showed her that she couldn't trust him. In fact, he'd need to earn her trust. She ran her tongue around her dry mouth, seeking moisture as she prepared to answer the mother in front of her.

"Camp ends at noon sharp. Today you should walk in to get your daughter, but tomorrow is when drop-off and pickup car pool begins." Brenna tucked an errant lock of hair behind her ear. She couldn't wait for car pool, as it meant less human interaction.

She turned and glared at the green door. Was Owen coming back at all? She shook off her irritation and focused on the petite mother in front of her, who had yet another simple question about car pool. The answers had started coming with a bit of ease. Maybe she could do this. Maybe she wasn't as weak as she thought. As she answered another question, her nerves stopped jangling.

Perhaps she wasn't mad at Owen. Maybe she was simply disappointed in her low self-esteem. She smiled at the mother-and-son team as they made their way to the pavilion. The picnic tables were filling up with children, eagerly awaiting the start of camp.

Now that vehicles had departed and campers were collected under the pavilion, she again glanced at Cora and Wade's home. Where was Owen? They had a camp to put on. Someone had to welcome the children, and he'd agreed to handle the big group announcements.

She gulped. With Owen missing, that someone was her.

She lifted her chin, pressed her damp palms against her hiking-pant-clad thighs and marched to the lectern in the pavilion, irritated that Owen had abandoned her for not only morning drop-off, but this as well.

As she strode across the space, the realization hit her that Owen couldn't help unless she came clean and told him about the break-in. If he was aware of her past, he might take his responsibilities more seriously and not leave her in the lurch, like he had this morning. Well, she certainly hoped that if he knew the truth, he would choose to support her.

Though talking about her past with someone who didn't already know would dredge up long-buried emotions. It was bad enough when she met with her counselor every week, but Owen? She dreaded the conversation she had to have with him. And soon.

She stepped up to the empty lectern. At her appearance, the sea of campers hushed and expectation lit up their faces. Lulu rested against her leg and Brenna gave the campers a wide smile, hoping to infect them with her own enthusiasm about the morning activities.

She could do this. After all, the kids were the reason she was here. And when the six weeks were over, after she'd proven herself, she'd figure out what she wanted to do with her life. Because she refused to let the past dictate her future.

Owen scrambled down the front steps and hurried toward the pavilion, slipping on his Stetson. What had he been thinking leaving Brenna like that? Especially after his mother had told him Brenna struggled with speaking to strangers. Sure, he was annoyed with Brenna because of the past, but he shouldn't have deserted her.

He kicked himself for rushing off to his mother's when he heard Evie crying, but the need to check on her had been instinctual. When he had arrived at his mother's, he picked Evie up and her crying had stopped. In an attempt to get back to camp quickly, he tried to hand the baby over to his mother, but he'd ended up feeding Evie a bottle, which took far longer than usual. He hadn't realized how hard it would be to leave his daughter all day.

As he strode toward the pavilion, a quick glance at the parking area showed him drop-off had ended. He made a wide berth around the building so as to not disrupt the welcoming session in progress. Brenna stood on the platform, clutching the podium with white knuckles, welcoming the campers. Lulu was pressed against her leg with a look of distress on her hair-covered doggie face. His heart ached for Brenna because their plan was for him to deal with parents during drop-off and pickup, as well as handle all the public speaking so she could stay in the background and keep things running smoothly.

He wanted to step up and take over for her, but that would be awkward. The next thing he knew, she cracked a joke and the kids laughed. Then she released them by groups as though she were a pro. Pride filled his core at how she handled herself.

The campers were organized into four groups and they'd rotate through a number of different activities. He and Brenna had set up the schedule purposely so they'd both be free for the first and fourth rotations to help volunteers and fix any issues as needed.

As the campers and volunteers dispersed, he made his way over to Brenna, who held on to her smile as though her life depended on it. Her knuckles were clasped by her sides and Lulu leaned against her, softly whining. The duo looked pathetic, and Owen felt horrible about deserting her.

"Good job," he said. He was proud of her for doing something she considered scary.

She turned to him, a hint of tears in her eyes, but then her emotions flashed anger. "Where were you?" she hissed.

He tried to explain about hearing Evie cry, but she interrupted him.

"You promised." Her hands were fisted by her side and Lulu backed off, almost like the dog thought her owner was upset with her. Brenna had every right to be upset because he had promised. But when he heard Evie's cry, he'd gotten all paternal and protective of his little one. Maybe because she didn't have a mother, and he constantly thought she felt abandoned. He continued to cling to guilt that he was at fault for Willow not being here to care for their baby.

"I'm sorry I left you high and dry earlier." The kids and volunteers had vanished, though he heard laughter and squeals off in the distance. She crossed her arms and gave him an *I can't believe you did that* look.

"What did your mother need help with?" Her lips squished together into a fine line. He tried to explain that he'd struggled to pull himself away from Evie, but with each sentence, he understood why she was agitated with him. He'd been irresponsible to leave her and then linger to feed Evie the bottle. Selfish even.

"I promise it won't happen again." He shouldn't worry over his baby, but after four months as her sole caretaker, letting go wasn't that simple. But his mother had the entire family checking in on Evie. She didn't need his help.

"Owen, I might not be the best person to help you run camp." Her face pinched with doubt while his mind whirred with her quick change of topic.

"No, Brenna, you're—"

"The kids deserve better than me. This is more than I can handle right now." It looked like her legs might buckle under her.

Since the campers were all in their groups handled by the volunteers, he and Brenna had about half an hour before they needed to be at their respective rotations. He inclined his head to the groupings of wooden picnic tables.

"Let's talk." Her teeth caught her bottom lip as though she were trying to figure out if she wanted to trust him. He got that. But more important, he couldn't have her back out. For some reason, having Brenna help manage camp was important to his mother. And these days, he'd do anything to keep his mother happy.

He strode to the tables. Lulu's nails clicked

on the concrete as she followed along, which meant Brenna had decided to join him. Maybe trust him. He settled on a bench seat, using the tabletop as a back rest, and placed his Stetson behind him. She slid to the far edge of the seat, still sharing the table, with Lulu at her feet.

"You can do this, Brenna. I saw how the campers reacted to you just now."

"You think?" Uncertainty swirled in her tone.

"Yes, absolutely."

In the distance, he spotted children brushing horses tied up to a long hitching post. He wanted to be sensitive to Brenna's concerns, but the next rotation would start soon and he was tasked with leading their horseback riding class. And Brenna had her baking rotation. Maybe he should have recommended that she stick with background stuff instead of teaching a baking class. But it was too late now.

"I didn't think it would be this hard," she said.

"You are doing a great job so far and I kind of need your organizational skills." His disorganization in just the past couple of days had surprised him. "I think we make a good team." Then he tossed her a crooked smile, hoping she'd stay on. Otherwise, his mother would kill him.

"Stop it, Owen. I know you don't want me and you probably don't need me." Lulu pushed her nose at Brenna and she encircled her dog's neck to give her a big hug.

"My mother told me that you need to help run camp. You have reasons, but she wouldn't explain."

She swallowed and started to play with her fidget rings as Jesse, one of their younger volunteers who helped with the horses, approached the pavilion.

Owen could kick himself for fighting her from the get-go. He figured he could handle camp on his own; after all, his mother had for years. But he was a lightweight compared to his mother. The more they planned for today, the more he realized he was out of his element. He needed Brenna's calm and organized presence beside him. Anyway, Brenna seemed to need camp. He wasn't sure why, but he could almost feel it in his bones. Except he was hesitant to let Brenna back into his life, even just a little—not after the ghosting and now her unwillingness to broach the topic.

"So I guess you deserve an explanation," she started. She blew out a breath as though she were about to tell him something big. Something important. But right then, Jesse stepped closer and cleared his throat.

"Excuse me, Mr. Owen," Jesse said. The boy had graduated high school in the spring and was excited to help out. "One of the horses is limping. What should we do?" Worry lines creased the boy's forehead.

This was a crinkle Owen hadn't prepared for. Their morning group was larger than he'd expected, so they planned to use every available hack. One lame horse was bad news.

"Hold that thought," he said to Brenna as he rose and rushed after Jesse toward the barn.

He wasn't sure what Brenna was about to say, but one thing he knew for sure—his mother wanted him and his ex-girlfriend to co-lead camp for her. Somehow Owen had to let go of his resentment toward Brenna so they could focus on smoothly running the camp together.

That way, he had a chance of mending his relationship with his parents.

Chapter Five

After the afternoon campers departed, Owen arrived at his parents' home to grab Evie so his mother could rest. When he rushed through the front door, the air conditioning was on blast, cooling the sweat droplets on his arms. He hurried to his room to pull on a fresh shirt, excited to cuddle with Evie while helping Brenna and the volunteers clean up and unpack any issues from the first full day of camp.

He returned to his mother in the living room. She smiled up at him, holding Evie on the couch, surrounded by diapers and bottles and chew toys. Man, he needed to pick this place up for her. He resettled his Stetson on his sweaty head and reached for Evie. Instead of being excited to see him, she eyed him and started crying. He froze, then cupped the back of his neck in frustration. She should know him by now. He'd been caring for her since birth. Was it possible that in the span of a few hours, she'd forgotten him?

He frowned and looked at his mother for reassurance. Maybe he should leave Evie with his mother and head back to camp for cleanup duty alone.

"Owen." The sympathy in his mother's voice washed over him. She had raised five kids, she'd know what to do. "Children, especially infants, are finicky. I mean, this morning she wanted nothing to do with me and looked at you like you hung the moon, remember?" His mother gazed at Evie, whose bottom lip stuck out while she stared at her father with displeasure. "It's the hat," his mother said quietly. "I bet she doesn't recognize you with that Stetson on."

He slipped his hat off and slid it onto the coffee table. Instantly, Evie's pout disappeared. Huh. That was weird. His mother gave him a smile and then turned to Evie and opened her mouth to speak.

"Dada," his mother said in a baby voice only women seemed to possess. Evie watched her grandmother's mouth moving and then peeked at him before trying to mimic what his mother was doing. Could she be processing that he was her father? Or maybe four-month-old kids couldn't process like that yet? He wasn't sure. But he believed Evie was pretty smart. In fact, she had defied the timelines in baby books by rolling from her tummy to her back at just three months. He glanced at his watch. He needed to get back to the pavilion to help clean up, but he didn't want to leave Evie in his mother's care for much longer.

He put his hands out and Evie leaned toward him. He and his mother made the handoff, then he settled his daughter on his hip.

"See, it was the hat," his mother said.

After his mother caught him up on the day, he slipped Evie into the pink front carrier Willow had been so excited to use and rushed over to join the volunteers picking up. He felt awful that he had taken so long to collect Evie. He'd have to do better with his time management in the future. Leaving Brenna with the bulk of things to handle wasn't fair, as she'd argued this morning.

He stepped into the shade of the pavilion as Brenna gathered the remnants of the afternoon campers' final activity—a water balloon fight. She'd turned from a pretty girl into a gorgeous and well-spoken woman in the last ten years. Not that he was looking. He admired her, especially because she was fighting back from some type of traumatic event in her past. But she was stronger than she realized. She'd win this fight. If only she'd believe in herself.

She stood and tucked a lock of hair behind her ear.

"Sorry that took so long," he said, adjusting Evie in the front carrier.

"Not a problem. The volunteers are gone, but I think we had a good day." She continued to pick up balloon fragments and drop them in a bucket, but he noticed her voice was strained. Had something happened while he was picking up Evie?

Lulu lay on the concrete, panting. It had been an exhausting day for everyone.

Evie kicked her legs and squealed, tossing him off-balance. He chuckled while he righted himself, then opened his mouth to make a joke about how much Evie loved the front carrier, but quickly closed it when he noticed Brenna's taut features. Was she upset he'd taken so long collecting his daughter?

He rubbed his forehead. No, earlier in the day they'd been interrupted. She had wanted to tell him something. Should he bring up the topic or would she?

"You are going to have to be here for morning and afternoon drop-offs," she said, her voice terse. "It's what you promised when we divided tasks."

"I already apologized for the morning drop-off fiasco. I promise I'll be there for it tomorrow."

She gave him a quick nod. "Good. But you need to be here for the afternoon one as well." Her chin was set in that firm, determined manner of hers. For some reason, he was the only one she seemed to have the guts to stand up to. He roughed a hand over his face. Though he was glad she had the gumption toward him, it had been a long day and he could use some down-time.

"We had talked about afternoon drop-off and I told you that I needed to help my mom with Evie during that time slot. Afternoon nap, re-member?"

"No. I told you that you could do it on Monday and then we'd regroup to discuss." Her voice was even and patient-sounding, probably her teacher voice. "This is the regroup." He cocked his head.

"And Evie is still going down for that final nap of the day. Nothing has changed in two days," he stated. "You may not understand, but naps are super important to staying on schedule and not being fussy and unenjoyable to be around in the evening." She frowned and put the bucket on a picnic table bench.

"Your mother raised five children. I think she can get Evie down for her nap." She crossed her arms and stared at him as though ready for a fight.

"Did something happen during the afternoon drop-off?" He hadn't heard grumblings of any kind.

"Yes. In fact, a father had a number of ques-tions." Her chin tilted up. "Hazel noticed and came over to help." She dropped her focus to the concrete beneath her feet as she tugged on the sleeves of her oversize shirt. Whatever happened had not been good. "Thankfully, I made it to the camp office before the panic attack started. That's the last thing the kids need to see."

Owen knew that worry over the campers seeing her have a panic attack was not the reason they were having this discussion. Something deeper was going on here. He stayed silent as he remembered his mother telling him that she'd promised Brenna to handle anything dealing with parents or male volunteers. When he'd asked her why, she'd told him that something had happened to bring Brenna back to Serenity, but it wasn't her story to share.

Had something happened that made dealing with men hard for Brenna? He wanted to apologize, but he wasn't sure for what. He felt bad that she'd been put in that situation, but he still had no idea what *that situation* was.

"I'm sorry I wasn't there." Brenna had been strong and courageous in high school. She now seemed defeated. Emotion clogged his throat. And he just knew it had something to do with the reason she'd returned to town.

She gave him a nod, then her gaze flicked to his face for a moment before she spoke. "I need to share something with you," she said in a soft voice.

"Is this about why you blocked my number when you left for that elite teacher summer camp after graduation?" He'd been hoping for an explanation.

She looked at him quizzically, then shook her head as though dismissing his question. The question that had been in the back of his mind for ten long years.

"No, Owen, it's about… Listen, the reason I blocked your number after graduation is irrelevant. You met and married Willow pretty quickly, so you must not have felt strongly toward me." He reared back as though he'd been slapped. What? He'd loved her. They'd talked about marriage and he believed they had a great relationship until she had blocked his calls for no reason. Anyway, they'd been broken up for over a year before he met Willow.

He wanted to retort, but Brenna raised her hand like a traffic cop. A serious expression he'd never seen before covered her face. Her mouth opened like a fish a couple of times before she spoke. Whatever she wanted to say was important. Maybe even emotional. So he kept quiet.

"Owen. If I don't speak, I think I'm going to lose my nerve." Her voice wobbled and her words came out in a rush. She gave her bottom lip a quick nibble and then took a cleansing breath. "One night when I was in Dallas, two men broke into my apartment." Lulu got to her feet and skittered over to Brenna, who reached down to hug the multicolored dog.

His stomach bottomed out at her shocking statement.

"Oh my, Brenna. That is horrible."

He thought he'd been living a nightmare the last few months. But Brenna had been too. He thanked God for Evie and pressed a kiss to his baby's fine hair. Thanks to Willow's persistence, he also had his family. His wife had filled the gaps for him, which made mending the relationship with his parents much easier to navigate.

Brenna kissed Lulu's furry head and a wave of guilt washed over him. He had taken for granted all the love and support he had behind him while she only had her dog and what appeared to be a lot of unhealed internal scars. And if her parents were still constantly arguing, then she didn't really have much of a support system other than the McCaws.

He gazed at the broken woman he had loved in high school, and his heart ached for her. He longed to rush to her and gather her in his arms, but that didn't feel right. Not with her leg tapping a staccato rhythm, and her grip tight on Lulu's neck. He sensed she needed to share her story. Whatever happened in the past had terrified her. And if she wanted to talk about it, he'd be here for her.

She returned to cleaning up from the water balloon fight that had ended their fun afternoon camp as though she didn't plan to finish telling him what had happened. But that contemplative look on her face told him that she was processing. She'd get there. He didn't want to push her, but his mind was wandering off in all sorts of terrible directions, imagining what had happened on that fateful night.

He rubbed the top of Evie's head. Out of respect, he would have to wait until Brenna was ready to continue.

To give her some time to compose herself, he grabbed a bucket and started collecting the colorful, damp latex pieces on the opposite side of the pavilion. But his gut twisted because, based on the frightened Brenna he'd seen recently, the ending of the story was likely grim.

Brenna picked up the last of the balloon fragments and set her litter bucket on the concrete. The way Owen's face had fallen when she'd told him about the two men just about did her in. Of course he cared. In high school, they'd been together for over a year, and good friends before that. They had even talked about a future.

Could she open up to him and share that horrible experience? She wasn't sure she had it in her today. Or any day.

But if they were going to work together for six weeks, he deserved to know. That way, he could support her.

Well, she hoped he'd choose to support her.

She looked across the pavilion at Evie strapped to his chest and felt the urge to touch the sweet, innocent baby. Maybe she'd get the fortitude she needed to continue her story. It was worth a try.

She weaved through the bulky picnic tables. Owen rose, his face serious yet comforting at the same time. She reached out to rub the baby's silky hair. The movement calmed Evie because she stopped moving her arms and stilled. Brenna whispered the child's name. Evie turned her head and Brenna ran a finger down the sweetheart's smooth cheek. So close to Owen, she could smell his unique outdoor aroma—hay and earth and fresh air.

"So you were in Dallas and two men broke in," he prodded in a soft voice. But even though he was being kind and nonjudgmental, she wasn't sure she could tell him. Talking in her sterile counselor's office was one thing, but this...

She stepped away from him and eyed the camp chairs that a volunteer had set up. She was exhausted from the day of running after little ones, but she was much too nervous to sit still. And since Owen was bouncing the baby, she opted to remain standing.

"Unless you don't want to talk about it, Brenna." When she gazed into his eyes, she saw the strength and compassion necessary to push forward. Their relationship may not have worked out, but he truly cared about her. And she needed to get this off her chest.

She reached for Lulu, encouraged by her emotional support dog's nearness. She wanted to move past the forced entry and attack and get back to her normal life. After a fulfilling day, even with the drop-off hiccup, she had to be brave and tell Owen so they could work together as a team. Not only for the kids, but for camp to become a place where she could heal.

She pressed her lips together, emotions rising to the surface. She shoved them down as she forced herself to open the faucet she had kept tightly closed and tell the story.

"When the two men broke in, I was stupid enough to confront them." What had she been thinking by grabbing that lamp and charging at them? What had she envisioned would happen? Of course, she'd hoped to clunk them on the head, subdue both of them and then call the police. But they were quick and snatched the lamp before she knew what was happening.

His eyes widened and his mouth gaped open in surprise. Like most people, he didn't know how to respond. Before she lost her courage, she pushed forward.

"And there was an assault." Key moments from that horrific night flashed through her mind. The scuffle. The moment she realized she'd literally been backed into a corner. Their evil faces. And so much more. She shuddered. Unthinkable things.

"Oh, Brenna." He touched her arm. Before he could try to hug her, she gave a little shake of her head. She didn't want anyone's pity, and the last thing she needed was to sink into his embrace. She had to straighten out her life before she got involved with anyone. Her emotional strength was of utmost importance, and leaning on a man right now wasn't an option. Besides, she was still mad at Owen.

He followed her lead and wrapped his arms around Evie instead of her. Even though Brenna didn't want a hug, she still missed the security of his arms around her. But staying apart was for the best. She was a "can do" kind of gal. She'd get through this and come out stronger on the other side.

Sadness filled Owen's chocolate brown eyes. At least she decided it was sadness and not pity. She hated pity.

"That must have been horrible," he said when she finished her tale.

Lulu leaned against her leg and Brenna reached for her relaxing fur. "It was terrifying." She blinked away the sudden tears, refusing to allow them to fall and for evil to win. "The assault left me in the hospital for a week and now affects how I deal with other people. It's the reason I have Lulu." The tension seemed to tumble from her body and her legs became wobbly. She dropped to her knees and encircled Lulu in a hug, allowing her dog to support her. She was grateful she'd had the courage to come clean to Owen. Now he'd understand her reticence about encountering strangers, especially men.

"I'm sorry you had to go through that, Brenna," he said. "Now I get why you wouldn't want to take on some of the tasks. So if there is any way I can support you…just say the word."

She gave him a single nod. Somehow, speaking about the past had allowed her to release a little more of the pain and fear she'd been clinging to for the past six months.

Evie fussed, so Owen started to bounce her, giving his full attention to his daughter.

Ten years ago, his role as a police officer had frightened her. It was the reason she'd gone radio silent on him. Yet today, she felt reassured, knowing she had someone on her side trained to fight off attacks.

But then she remembered her counselor's plan for her to build independence and strength this summer by facing people and situations she couldn't control. She'd have to be careful not to rely on Owen.

She took another step away to distance herself from him and looked up at her garage apartment longingly. Right now, all she wanted to do was bake dozens of cookies, maybe dig into that tart recipe she'd been perfecting. Or perhaps simply curl up on the extra-long couch and take a nap. With large oaks surrounding the space, her apartment was like a tree house. Just walking in the door calmed her.

Suddenly exhausted, she collapsed in one of the camp chairs. The day must have finally caught up with her.

She gazed up at Owen, who was making silly faces at his baby, and her breath caught. What if Cora asked her to move out of the garage apartment so that Owen could move in? Her heart thudded. Where would she go? Other than the McCaws, she didn't have anyone else who cared about her. Her time in Dallas had been like a vacuum. She had no idea how years passed and she hadn't found a solid girlfriend group.

At this point, returning to her childhood home

would do more damage than good, since she'd heard her parents were arguing now more than ever. No, that wasn't an option. She pushed away the fear of being booted from her feels-like-home apartment and returned her thoughts to their discussion.

"I'm sorry I wasn't here for drop-off earlier," he said. "I can help with the parents. I can help you through this tough time."

Her stomach clenched that she needed help. Though he was trying to be kind, she hated that she couldn't do this on her own.

A dusty dually pulled into the parking area. Her mood flipped to thrilled when she spotted Emma McCaw driving. She'd become friends with the mother of triplets in the past few months. Emma, the wife of Owen's brother Carter, owned a goat farm as well as a family store where she sold all sorts of things, including baked goods. Owen's sister-in-law climbed out of the truck. When she spotted Brenna, she gave a little wave and made a beeline for her.

"Just the person I was looking for," Emma said as she stepped under the shade of the pavilion. They hugged, but Brenna could tell her friend was flustered.

"What's going on? Is everything okay?" After that deep conversation with Owen, Brenna was elated to concentrate on something other than what had happened six months ago.

"I don't know what to do. I promised cupcakes for an event that Hazel Murray is organizing. I didn't think it'd be a big deal to add a couple dozen cupcakes to my baking order with Myrtle, but she says she doesn't have time," Emma spoke quickly as she twisted her fingers in worry. "Maybe I should just call Hazel and tell her I can't do it, but the event is in the morning. I don't know what—"

"Emma, it's okay." Finally, a topic Brenna had mastery over. "I can make something for you."

She turned her worried face to Brenna with such hope. "You can?"

Adrenaline flooded Brenna's system at the thought of another paying baking job. Well, it sounded like a paying job. Either way, it'd be fun.

"I can do cupcakes. I have a yummy red velvet cupcake that I make with a cream cheese frosting. It is delectable." But Emma's worried look came back.

"Three dozen red velvet might be too overpowering," Emma said, uncertainty covering her face. "I'm sorry. At this point, I'll take anything. Red velvet would be great."

"Hold on," Brenna said, turning all businesslike. She hadn't realized her friend wanted a variety. She could do that. With Emma all flustered, she'd just tell her what she'd bake instead of giving options. "How about a dozen chocolate cupcakes with a cappuccino buttercream frosting? A dozen red velvet with a cream cheese frosting. And a dozen lemon raspberry cupcakes with strawberry buttercream frosting. Would that work?"

"You can do that?" The hope was back on her friend's face. Brenna smiled.

"I can," she assured Emma. "Now, I usually pipe the frosting pretty high for events, about the height of the cupcake. Does that sound okay or would you like it shorter?"

"Oh, my, that sounds so gourmet and absolutely perfect. I think I'm going to need to provide forks." They chuckled.

"Actually, I have petite disposable forks that work nicely," Brenna said. "The smaller utensil allows the ladies to savor the dessert." Emma was excited about the petite forks and wanted them. Then they agreed on when Emma would pick them up in the morning and the price. Before she left, Emma gave her brother-in-law a hug and Evie a kiss on the top of her sweet head. Then she rushed to her truck with a thankful wave.

Brenna was going to be paid for this job. She

grinned. Seemed people were paying her as though she were a professional, and she liked that.

"Congratulations," Owen said. Evie looked sleepy, like she might nod off at any second.

"Thank you. I'm going to check out my supplies and make sure I don't need to make a grocery run. See you tomorrow." She hustled up the staircase to her apartment, Lulu following, and whipped open her pantry door. She took a quick inventory and decided she had everything she needed right here. The opportunity to bake for Emma took the sting away from the hard conversation with Owen.

She washed her hands and then started pulling the necessary ingredients onto the butcher-block island, excited to do some focused baking this evening. It would be a good way to decompress after the first day of camp.

But as she contemplated the exchange with Owen from earlier about drop-off, her breath temporarily bottled up in her chest. She hated that she wasn't strong enough to stand on her own. She released a frustrated sigh, then pulled the butter from the fridge and set it on the counter to thaw.

A thought popped into her mind—what if she was stronger than she believed?

Hope niggled in her core, especially because she'd handled the morning drop-off as well as greeting the morning campers without a panic attack. In fact, volunteers had commended her. So maybe she was actually in the process of healing.

Other than the glitch with the father this afternoon, of course. But if Owen kept his promise, she wouldn't get caught off guard like that again.

And Emma's look of appreciation at Brenna's offer to bake the cupcakes had given her confidence as well.

She smiled at her sudden optimism. Maybe her past trauma would not always define her.

Chapter Six

During the second morning of camp, a grin crossed over Owen's face. So far, just a few hiccups. The sun shone brightly again today, so he tilted his Stetson lower on his forehead. Because of the heat, they had kept the campers in shaded areas as much as possible. He strode over to the covered pavilion as cows behind the fence mooed at him.

He nudged some picnic tables back into place, preparing for a swarm of campers to join together as a group one final time before pickup. He still struggled with digesting what Brenna had told him about the break-in and assault. His heart ached for her. The events explained her brokenness and now he felt horrible for making a stink this past weekend when she had asked him to take on certain tasks. Clearly, she'd been trying to avoid dealing with strangers, especially adult men. Now he understood why.

The kids started rushing the space, and he held his palm out for a high five from a fifth grader who had glommed on to him during his horse-back riding rotation. Jackson stopped in front of him and proceeded to talk about his favorite part of the morning before his friends joined him, then they wandered off, chatting among themselves.

Owen smiled at how many of the campers were having such a great time and making new friends. There were a couple that seemed either to be left out or feel left out. He made a mental note to discuss those campers with the other volunteers later on because they likely needed some help to assimilate socially.

Brenna stepped into the pavilion, her pretty blond hair piled atop her head. Perhaps her goal was to stay cool, but the hairdo highlighted her high cheekbones, her cute nose and the delicate shape of her lips. Did anyone else notice how gorgeous she was at this moment? He looked around, but no one else seemed to be staring at her, so Owen tried to move his gaze elsewhere. Lulu heeled beside her as Brenna fanned her rosy face with her hand and laughed at something a volunteer said to her. He pushed his momentary attraction away, happy to see her having a lighthearted moment.

A few minutes later, cars began to line up in front of the pavilion, instead of parking in the lot. Parents, mostly mothers, sat in their cars while volunteers walked children to minivans and dual-cab pickup trucks that had colorful sheets displayed on their dashboard with their child's name written on it.

"What's going on?" he asked Brenna. Her smile faded as she turned to him. The flash of annoyance in those sky blue eyes landed on him with the force of a physical blow. She reached for Lulu. Had he used an angry tone? He hadn't meant to sound irritated, but he was confused because in all the years he'd helped his mother, parents had walked in to gather their children.

"Didn't you pay attention during the volunteer meeting on Sunday?" She gave Lulu several pats, and he immediately felt bad that he had caused her enough distress to need her emotional support dog. But he still had no idea what was happening. "We discussed that parents now have the option of parking and walking in to pickup like usual, or forming a car pool line where we will shepherd their child to them."

Before he could form a comeback, a volunteer called her over to a minivan with a question. Since Brenna knew the driver, he didn't tag along, but he did pay close attention. When she smiled and then chuckled, he released the worried breath he'd been holding.

Though he was still processing the horror she had gone through, somehow protecting her and her emotional healing were of utmost importance to him.

In a way, he struggled to believe Brenna Park was back in his life. And that they were deeply intertwined for the next six weeks.

By the time Brenna returned to his side, the children were gone and the parking lot was a flurry of gravel dust.

But this car pool line boggled his mind. For twenty-five years, his mother had instructed parents to park their vehicle and walk their children into camp, then pick them up the same way. What would she think? He felt bad for Brenna, because he knew camp was some type of emotional test for her, but once he informed his mother, she'd probably drop Brenna like a hot potato.

"I'm sorry for upsetting you earlier, Brenna, but this is a big change." He tried to be as gentle as possible. He considered it a win when she didn't reach for Lulu. His mother would be displeased with this turn of events. His goal this summer was to make up with his parents, not disappoint them. He contemplated the car pool change, but was unable to come up with a positive.

"My mother believes having the parents walk their children in is a great opportunity for them to connect with other parents," he told her, trying to not sound harsh. But the tight line her lips formed told him clearly that she was unhappy with him. "Also, the volunteers were able to communicate necessary things to parents during this time." He turned toward his parents' house, intending to check on Evie. But it would also give him the perfect opportunity to let his mother know, without making Brenna anxious, that Brenna had made another big change.

Brenna touched his elbow and tugged him back. As he moved into her personal space, the breeze lifted her fragrance to him, reminding him of their high school days together. But when he took in her features, they held a fierceness he hadn't seen yet this summer. Even though she appeared upset with him, he felt like cheering because *this* was the Brenna he remembered. A woman who stood up for herself. The home invasion has stolen that, but he could see glimpses of the confident Brenna he knew.

"You had your turn, now I get mine," she stated, her chin set firm. "Your mother and I spoke at length about this change, along with every change we've made to *her* summer camp." The emphasis on his mother and the way Brenna glared at him had him kicking himself. He'd been so fearful his parents wouldn't accept him back into the fold that he'd assumed the worst of Brenna. Of course, she'd gotten approval from his mother. That was probably why his mother had named her a co-leader this year.

"This change is a request but not a requirement," she continued. "For car pool riders, a half sheet of paper is now sent home to communicate anything necessary. Parents can walk their children in, but the car pool scenario gives children more hands-on time at camp and parents a little more time to themselves."

Ah, that actually made sense. A lot of sense.

"I'm sorry, Brenna. Obviously, I jumped the gun, not understanding all the details."

"Apology accepted," she said, but her voice was still strained, as though she was still unhappy with his reaction. "But Owen, you were about to run to your mother again, because you thought I'd done something without her approval." She straightened. The bravery in her stance made Owen want to applaud her strength, but he held back. "We need to work as a team. That means talking to each other about issues that arise."

"Noted." He made sure to keep his face neutral. What he really wanted was to grin at Brenna's huge achievement. He was so proud of her. But since she was serious and upset with him, he tamped down his excitement.

Even though he'd been hurt by Brenna, he still missed her. Missed the future they never got to have. He shook his head, upset he'd have thoughts like that about anyone other than Willow. His chest gave a tight squeeze at his betrayal of his wife.

"I let the volunteers leave for lunch, so let's disinfect the bounce house before the afternoon campers arrive." She grabbed a bucket of supplies and strode away. He jogged to keep up.

"Listen, I noticed the volunteer parents are not in their child's group." They reached the bounce house. "When I was a kid, I always enjoyed when a friend had a parent who volunteered because we got to interact with them."

Brenna huffed out a frustrated sigh. "Owen, parents these days tend to be helicopter parents. It's simply healthier to separate kids from volunteer parents. And before you question me, yes that change was also approved by your mother." She handed him a cloth, then started spraying the areas where the morning campers had played. He followed her and wiped the spray down with his dry cloth.

The attack may have stolen her confidence, but it hadn't changed her impressive intelligence. Before long, they were done disinfecting the bounce house and parted ways for lunch. She went to her garage apartment. He went to his parents' home to stuff a quick lunch down while he gave his mother a brief break from Evie before the next set of campers arrived.

After the lunch break, he strode down his parents' porch before any of the afternoon campers arrived and stationed himself well in front of Brenna, as though blocking her from any possible messiness.

Though he was happy to do it, protecting Brenna meant he'd be spending more time with her. And that conflicted with his plan to stay far away because of his long-held hurt.

Anyway, he should focus on the present, which meant mending his relationship with Brenna so they could peacefully work together. But would the unknown reason she ghosted him always create tension between them? He sure hoped not.

Except the unexpected attraction he'd been feeling toward her today surprised him. What was that all about? He wasn't sure, but he needed to make sure that spending time together wouldn't rekindle any romance.

Because that was the last thing he wanted.

In the small building connected to the open-air pavilion, Brenna swept the last of the debris into the dustpan, then dumped the contents into the garbage can. The room she used for camp cooking classes was cozy but big enough for the amount of kids in her rotation. She released a satisfied sigh, thrilled with how the classes were going after just two full days. She stuffed the moments into her memory bank to savor for later. Lulu lay at a down-stay in the doorway, watching intently.

Brenna smiled at her dog and straightened, feeling the loose hem of her Bermuda shorts against her bare leg. With her usual long sleeves and sweatpants, she'd been uncomfortably hot this morning. So over the lunch break, she'd changed clothes. Still all black, but above the knee shorts and a thinner, short-sleeved shirt. Except now that she wasn't outdoors in the heat and humidity, she felt vulnerable. She tugged the shorts down so they touched her knees.

Would she ever regain her confidence? She shook off the notion. Surely if she kept at it, she'd return to normal. Or at least a new normal that felt more like herself.

She scanned the room to verify there was no more food on the floor, then released Lulu with a verbal command. Her sweet dog took off, nose to the ground, to check her work. When she licked a few spots, Brenna chuckled at her antics.

"I'm rewarding you with a peanut-butter-filled Kong as soon as we get home." With all this tempting food at her level, Lulu had been so patient today.

Brenna turned her attention to the tables

smeared with colored frosting. This might take a while, as today the teens had frosted the cookies they'd made yesterday. This morning was a mess with the little ones, but not as bad as this. Had she turned her back to kids having a food fight or something?

She chuckled and glanced out the window. Owen was striding past the building with a couple of other volunteers; likely they were done with their afternoon cleanup.

Her lighthearted mood turned sour at his presence. She was still irked about his reaction toward the new pickup and drop-off procedures. She couldn't believe he'd jumped to the conclusion that she'd unilaterally made the decision without Cora's approval. As if.

Sure, he had apologized, but it was obvious he didn't trust her because he wasn't treating her like a partner, more like an outsider who had no right to be in charge. But since Cora had set them up as co-leaders, she was determined to work like a team.

Lulu groaned and nudged her. Brenna looked down and patted her dog's head. "I'm okay. He just irritates me." Lulu gave her a goofy smile and Brenna sent her to her bed. She had to stop relying on her dog and start living.

At least Owen was more attentive to her aversion of interacting with strangers, specifically male parents. He'd been like a security guard today. And she kind of liked it.

She dragged the trash can over to the table and started wiping the tables down. "I did stand up to him, though, didn't I?" Though Lulu didn't respond, Brenna remembered the moment she'd pulled on his elbow to stop him from running to his mother. Again. At least she'd had the guts to speak her mind, without spending hours agonizing over it.

He had tipped his Stetson low over his head as she spoke her mind, looking more handsome than a man ought to. The corners of his adorable lips had turned up as though he were trying not to smile while she lit into him. Why could she envision him so clearly?

"Hey, there." Owen interrupted her daydreaming as his broad shoulders filled the doorway. Lulu popped up from her bed and rushed over for some loving. Owen grinned and reached down to tousle her head. Lulu sat and pressed into him as he started to massage her ears. Her favorite.

If it were the nineteenth century, Brenna would swoon. But she held herself back and instead averted her gaze from the happy duo.

The last thing she needed was out-of-control emotions. She twirled her fidget ring a few times and then forced herself to continue to clean the goo off the tables.

"Can I help?"

She looked around the room at the immense amount of colorful frosting caked on the tables. "Sure." She nodded to the roll of paper towels.

He grabbed a fistful and started wiping down the table beside her. He was so close it kind of made her nervous. Or maybe interested, she wasn't sure.

"I like your new attire," he said, eyes focused on the table he was cleaning.

She hugged herself. He'd noticed? The feel of her bare arms against her fingertips felt strange. For six months she'd worn long sleeves and sweatpants in an attempt to hide. She jutted her chin out. Well, not anymore. She wasn't going to allow fear to win.

He moved to the next table, and she wondered if she was supposed to reply to his comment. It was one thing to wear shorts and a T-shirt, but there was no way she was going to chat with him about it. She gazed at him. His respectful manner of avoiding eye contact while making the comment made her appreciate him even more. Instead of responding, she blurted out the only thing she could think of.

"So, tell me about Willow," she said, then cringed. Why had she just asked that? He was still mourning. She was about to take her question back when she saw a smile flit across his face.

"She was kind and had a friend stationed on my base," he said. "We met about two years after I joined the military."

"That seems quick," she blurted. Man, could she just keep her mouth closed?

"It wasn't quick at all, Brenna," he shot back, a frown on his lips.

She twirled her fidget ring a few more times. She shouldn't be so judgmental. But she hadn't dated seriously since they had broken up, though that wasn't his fault. He had set the bar high.

Before she could formulate a response, an apology really, he spoke. His voice sounded a bit agitated.

"Anyway, you haven't answered my question about why you blocked my number." He glared at her.

The room felt topsy-turvy. He'd come in wanting to help, and she'd upset him.

"It had nothing to do with you as a person." It hadn't. It was about his career, but he didn't need to know that. "I'm sorry about how I handled cutting off our communication. I was wrong. I should have had a conversation with you." She kept wiping the already spotless tabletop, not wanting to see the disappointment in his eyes.

Maybe she should just come clean about why she blocked his calls. Trust that God would work it out. But she'd held so tightly to her fear—that Owen would have hurt her if they stayed together—she was almost afraid to bring the truth to the light.

Was this an example of relying on self and not on God? She and Cora had chatted after the sermon on Sunday and all Brenna could think of since then was that verse in Hebrews about being content with what you have and that God would never leave or forsake her. She clung to that promise now more than ever.

"It's so cool to see you baking with the older kids," Owen said, effectively changing the topic. Phew. "You seem to really like it."

"Well, we don't have an oven here, so we don't bake," she reminded him, thrilled to chat about baked goods. "But we do whip up batter that I bake in my apartment and then we can decorate, which is why this place is such a mess today." She grinned at the sweet memories she and the teens had made today decorating cookies.

"I can tell you enjoy baking. I mean, the stuff you make that I get to eat." He licked his lips and patted his flat stomach. "You are gifted."

Her cheeks warmed with his praise. "I just follow recipes."

"But I thought you loved teaching." He leaned

across the table and gave her a quizzical look. The way he gazed at her made her think he really cared. She cherished the moment because these past six months had made her feel so alone. It was nice to have her friend back.

"Oh, I do, but I'm not sure if I want to go back to teaching." She tossed the used paper towel in the trash and tried to ignore the look of appreciation sitting on Owen's face. "Baking calms me and makes me happy, but I don't think baking will pay my rent."

"That's why you work at the bakery every Saturday." Approval, maybe even respect, covered his face. Being seen as more than a victim felt surprisingly good. Maybe she *was* moving on with her life.

"Yes. In fact, Edith has mentioned she's close to retiring." The bakery owner had told her this the other day as though Brenna would jump at the chance to purchase the business.

His eyes lit up. "That's exciting. I can see you as a business owner. You've run this place like a tight ship, even if it's only been a few days."

She shook her head and put her hands up to stop him. "No, Owen, I don't have the funds to buy the bakery." Frankly, the thought of owning a business and managing employees didn't appeal to her, but she didn't want to disappoint Edith. "I don't know what I'm going to do when summer is over. I've been praying for clarity. But I might have to return to teaching because I can't keep living here rent-free."

Lulu must have sensed her unease because she trotted across the room and pressed against Brenna's leg. But for some reason, her dog didn't give her the immediate relief she usually did.

"You okay?" Owen asked. He was so close she could smell the mint from the gum he was chewing.

She nodded. She welcomed his encouragement. She truly did. But talking about her future brought back the truth—she had no idea what she was going to do with her life.

Unfortunately, she had lost her passion for teaching and gained a passion for baking, which was a hobby.

And she wasn't like Owen—she didn't have a family to lean on. Her parents, though in Serenity, constantly argued and put themselves ahead of her. It would be a mistake to think they could emotionally help her when they didn't have it together themselves.

Lulu leaned closer. Brenna focused on her emotional support dog, grateful for Lulu, but she wished she didn't rely on the dog so much.

She sighed at her predicament—no paying job and no real plan for the future.

On top of that, Brenna should really move

out of Cora's apartment when camp ended. The woman had been more than hospitable, but now Cora had a widowed son and his baby back home. The least Brenna could do was find somewhere else to live by the end of camp.

So, instead of the monumental task of figuring out a career, she should also try to focus on finding a new home.

Though she wasn't sure how she could possibly accomplish that without an income.

Chapter Seven

On the second Friday afternoon of camp, Brenna realized there hadn't been any major issues—two full weeks. Praise God! She hummed as she stood in the shade of the pavilion, monitoring pickup. With the sun bright again today and the heat index close to one hundred degrees, they'd played a lot of water games and stayed in the shade as much as possible.

Campers rushed past her, their sneakers tapping against the concrete as they scurried to their assigned lines. By now, volunteers had caught on to Brenna's need to remain in the background when parents arrived, so they had stepped up their contribution during those times of the day. Almost like they were being protective of her. Another reason her decision to remain in Serenity was sound. Under the canopy of the pavilion, she scratched the scruff of Lulu's head. The dog tipped up her nose, clearly enjoying the attention.

Ashley, the teen she'd clicked with earlier while

mixing ingredients for a bundt cake, rushed up for a quick hug. Brenna's chest gave a tight squeeze at the sweet gesture.

"Enjoy waterskiing this weekend," Brenna said as she hugged the girl back.

"I will." Ashley grinned and then hurried to the family minivan.

As the girl slipped into the vehicle, a smile split Brenna's lips. The experience of running camp, along with meeting girls like Ashley, had helped restore some of her confidence.

One by one, the vehicles in line for pickup drove off. Parents loved the car pool change. A couple of mothers parked and walked toward the pavilion. Mrs. Hudson, the mother of teenagers Bella and Arielle, strode toward Brenna with purpose, a frown on her face.

As panic bubbled up from within, she reached down to pet Lulu. Her dog leaned against her and awarded her a look that gave Brenna the confidence she needed for what might turn into a conflict-ridden conversation. She prayed for a clear head and kind words.

"Just the person I was looking for," Mrs. Hudson stated as she stopped about a foot away, a little too close for comfort. But Brenna made a point to stand her ground.

"How can I help you, Mrs. Hudson?" She wanted to lean down and snuggle Lulu for reassurance, but instead, she maintained eye contact with the frowning woman.

"It has come to my attention that Bella and Arielle are expected to brush their horses and tack them up." She wrinkled her nose as though disgusted with the thought of her girls dirtying their hands. "We pay extra at Serenity Stables so they don't have to do those mundane chores." Brenna didn't think it possible, but the woman lifted her nose a little higher in the air.

Brenna considered her options. She could give in to the woman and just ask Owen to prep the horses for the girls, like his brother and sister-in-law provided at their equine facility, Serenity Stables. If she asked, surely he'd do that for her. But it wouldn't be fair to the other teenagers. Anyway, the whole point of caring for and tacking the horses was about the experience and learning responsibility. The girls might not always have a wealthy mother to pay other people to do chores for them.

Before she could say a word, she felt, rather than saw, Owen stepping up beside her. She appreciated how protective he had become of her, but she needed to start handling situations on her own instead of relying on others. Otherwise, she'd never heal. Never get back to living her life. And she hated being weak.

"I appreciate that Trisha and Walker have that

option for boarders," she said about the owners of Serenity Stables. "But here at Victory Youth Camp, our goal is to immerse the campers in experiences." Her mouth was dry. Though she needed a sip of water, she forced herself to push forward and handle this altercation with Mrs. Hudson. "Part of the horseback riding rotation includes the care and feeding of the horses, as well as tacking and untacking. If you'd prefer them to be moved to a different rotation, we can do that. There is room in the baking class."

"Well, I never…"

Her response wasn't clear to Brenna at all. "Are you saying you'd like me to switch the girls to the baking rotation?"

"Absolutely not," Mrs. Hudson said, then turned on her heel and strode back to her luxury vehicle, which probably cost more than Brenna could make as a schoolteacher in three years.

Brenna shook her head at the audacity of the woman. Thankfully, Bella and Arielle seemed like down-to-earth girls who appeared to enjoy not only tacking their horses, but helping others as well. But she hoped she hadn't offended Mrs. Hudson.

"Good job," Owen stated from right behind her. She could feel his breath on her neck. If she were to turn, they'd be close enough to kiss.

Her eyes popped open. What had brought that thought to mind?

Just to be safe, she took a step forward before turning. She didn't want to bump into him. That would be embarrassing. She tried not to inhale his aftershave mixed with the scent of horse and outdoors, but was unsuccessful.

"I'm impressed with how you handled Mrs. Hudson," he said, a twinkle of appreciation in his eyes. Stubble lined his jaw, making her want to reach out and touch his chin. She fisted her hands and glued them to her side. His sweet demeanor drew her to him, and it didn't hurt that he was easy to look at with that dark hair and tanned skin. "Must be your schoolteacher skills, because you are amazing at neutralizing conflict."

Her cheeks warmed at his kind words. Yes, Lulu and her weekly counselor sessions were helping her heal. But her reaction to Mrs. Hudson? That was confirmation she was moving in the right direction.

"A month ago I never would have been able to handle that situation," she said.

"Well, then, I'm doubly impressed." Owen's eyes sparkled at her. He wore a pair of dark-wash jeans, cowboy boots and a slate blue polo shirt that highlighted his dark eyes every bit as much as his impressive biceps. She gave herself a virtual headshake. He had chosen a career that made him run to danger. Every day. She couldn't take a chance at allowing herself to fall for him again. Not that she was in the headspace to trust a man again anyway.

They moved to the bounce house, she with a bucket of cleaning products. She started spraying, and he followed, wiping the vinyl dry.

"We should fold this up and stick it in the corner of the pavilion for the weekend," she stated.

"Is it gonna rain?"

She nodded. They worked in tandem for a few minutes, then Owen broke the silence.

"My mother mentioned you are going to call Serenity home now. Same here."

"Shouldn't be too hard to find police work somewhere around here. At least in Love Valley," she stated.

"Probably. But I'm looking for something other than police work now that I'm a single father." He wiped the glistening spray down as he moved closer and closer to her.

Shock settled in her core at these revelations. She started spraying again and moved away to figure out what he'd just said. He was not only staying in Serenity but also seeking a safer occupation.

She turned the corner and breathed, knowing

she had a couple of moments to herself before he caught up with her.

She scrutinized his actions since they'd reconnected and the realization hit that he wasn't the risk-taker he'd been in high school. Yes, he was still a police officer, but he seemed different somehow. Of course, ten years had passed; they were both different and more mature. Both walked challenging paths. But the memory of everything that had happened after her father's injury stuck in her mind, the reason she had blocked Owen's calls.

He rounded the corner and grabbed a dry towel from her bucket.

"What are you going to do for a career?" she asked.

He spread his arms wide, and a slow smile spread across his handsome face. "I have no idea."

She knew how that felt. Part of her wished teaching still appealed to her because that was the easy solution.

"One thing I'm interested in is mentoring underprivileged teens," he said, "like I did back in North Carolina at our church. As a volunteer, though, not for a job or anything." His face lit up as he discussed the mentoring. Clearly, it had fulfilled him.

She smiled. His passion intrigued her. She jerked her head back.

"You okay?" he asked.

No. She wasn't okay. Not at all.

"I just realized something I need to do in the office." She grabbed the spray bottle and bolted. This curiosity about him and the glimmer of attraction she felt were not good.

She needed to focus on herself. Get through camp successfully. Find a job and a new home. She was in the throes of healing from the trauma of the assault, so that should be her focus. Not a man.

She heaved herself into the office chair. Lulu trotted over and pushed her nose against her bare leg, but she ignored her dog because she had a whopper of a problem.

She was attracted to Owen again. Dread balled in her stomach.

Why had she so easily fallen back into the trap of leaning on him?

Well, no more. She couldn't allow childish romantic emotions to crop back up and cloud her judgment.

That evening, Owen bounced Evie, who was asleep in his arms, and scanned his parents' living room. He grimaced at his recent invasion into their empty-nest lives. Living with his parents as a twenty-eight-year-old widower had never been his plan. Sure, they enjoyed having Evie, as well as their other grandchildren around, but having them visit and then go home was one thing. The garage apartment wasn't an option, but now that he knew about Brenna's past, he understood why his mother had been so generous with the space. And Brenna seemed to be healing, almost right in front of his eyes. Her transformation was miraculous to see.

"As soon as camp is over, I'll find a job and move out," he informed his mother. "I'm sorry to be imposing like this. You know, after…" She looked up from the romance novel she was reading in her pajamas. Her steaming nightly tea sat on the end table close by.

"After what?" she prodded. But she looked like she knew exactly what he was talking about. He squirmed like he had as a teenager.

His father was in the back room, watching sports in his favorite recliner. Well, by now he was likely fast asleep and wouldn't hear a word of this conversation.

"The years of limited contact." He held Evie a little tighter. Just saying the words squeezed his chest. He'd allowed a chasm to develop between him and his parents, and he had no idea how to fix it. Helping with summer camp was a start, but it sure wasn't enough. He pressed a soft kiss to the top of his daughter's head, her downy soft hair tickling his lips.

"But you were planning to reach out, Willow told me."

He pulled his head back in surprise. "She did?"

"Yes." His mother tucked a bookmark into her novel and laid it aside. "I think you made the conflict with your father and me into a bigger thing than it was. I'm not going to say I wasn't hurt, but having you here these past few weeks has been good for this momma's heart."

"But you guys were disappointed in me. I understood that."

"Now, son, that's not true." Her features held love and patience, but there had to be disappointment and hurt in there somewhere.

"You both thought I should stay here and take up ranching with Dad."

"No, Owen. We wanted all of you kids to do exactly what you wanted. Just because your father is a rancher and your grandfather was a rancher didn't mean any of you would ranch." Evie made a noise and his mother gave her a loving smile. The smile of a proud grandmother. "Dad knew that. He didn't want to foist his dream on any of you. No, Owen. At the time, we felt like you had made a snap decision to join the military. We were concerned you hadn't fully thought it out. Frankly, we wanted you in a safer field."

"Well, I couldn't become a police officer until I turned twenty-one, so I figured the next best thing was military police in the army." Yet now he was contemplating another field. To be safe for Evie. How ironic was that?

"Right, but joining the military at eighteen without talking to us? As a parent, that was worrisome. But what was more concerning was how you stopped communicating with the family." She reached for her mug of tea and wrapped her fingers around the warm ceramic. "You had every right to join the military, and we are sorry if we made you think we didn't support you. Because we always have."

Light dawned as Owen realized he was the one who had allowed the distance between them. He had misconstrued their well-meaning advice, and contorted it to believe they thought he was too immature to join the military. But he'd been wrong. In truth, his parents only had his best interests at heart. He had pushed them and their concerns away. For years.

His mother continued. "I'm so glad I've been able to communicate with Willow so freely over the years. She was like a daughter to me." Her eyes became glossy and his throat clogged at how many people were affected by the loss of Willow. Not just him.

"She felt like you were a bonus mom to her. She loved you." He blinked away the sudden tears. Evie started squirming. "I'm going to put this nugget to bed so she can stretch out in her crib." He settled beside his mother to give her a hug good-night and his mother reached her arms around his neck and squeezed. She held on for a long moment, and he smelled the spearmint in her herbal tea before she released him. He kissed her cheek and then headed upstairs, thankful they'd had this talk. Though he had hurt his parents, his mother especially, from the lack of communication, it seemed like the relationship with them was mending. And his mother was looking him in the eye these days, which was a good start.

He settled Evie in her crib, on her stomach like she liked, and pulled a thin blanket over her. Lights shone in the window. As he twisted the blinds closed, he noticed the string lights in the camp pavilion were on full power. He slipped out of the room to head to the pavilion.

He tried to tell himself Brenna was just his co-leader, and he wanted to see if she was out there and needed help. But his insides were humming with the chance to spend more time with her.

After he stepped onto the front porch, he spotted her moving picnic tables and dashed over.

"Let me help." He jumped in and kind of took over, smelling her shampoo as they neared. Why hadn't he thought of doing this before he left this afternoon? Brenna probably had a ton of things to do. She was dressed in a form-fitting top coupled with capri slacks and cute sandals, and he wondered if she had a date. After all, it was Friday night.

"Is Evie down for the night?" Lulu raced over to her with a yellow tennis ball and dropped it at Brenna's feet. She giggled, picked it up and then threw it across the yard. Lulu dashed after it.

He lifted the baby monitor clipped to his jeans pocket. "Yep. She always sleeps well for the first four hours. After that, it's hit or miss."

Brenna smiled and leaned against the brick wall, letting him move the remaining tables back. "Camp is going well even without Cora at the helm, don't you think?"

He agreed with her, then pushed the last table into place, surprised at how far he'd come in just a few weeks. For the most part, he was enjoying working with Brenna. And surprisingly, the innovative ideas she had were going over well with the parents.

"How are the Bible lessons going?" she asked while walking over to the cornhole game.

He couldn't stop the grin from splitting his face as he followed her. He was downright giddy about the teaching, especially the older kids. "Wanna play?" He lifted his chin toward the game.

She shrugged and picked up a blue, pellet-filled bag. "I take it from the look on your face that they are going well?" She waited until he had picked up the red bags and stood across from her. Lulu returned with her ball, panting, and lay near Brenna.

"Remember when we used to play this?" He lobbed his bag, and it almost hit the hole, but then it slid clear off the board. "Man," he said, frustrated at his toss.

She giggled. "Yes, I remember playing. I also recall how competitive you were. Maybe still are." She threw her first one, and it hit the board, right below the hole. She screwed up her face as though upset.

"I see *your* competitive streak is intact."

"Ha ha. So, tell me about the Bible teaching." They continued to play, both rusty with their technique.

"I love it. And the kids, especially the older ones, seem to be receptive." Two weeks of preparing and teaching Bible lessons had actually taught Owen that he didn't know as much about the Bible as he'd thought.

"I'm so excited for you." She took her turn, and the bag went into the hole. She danced around for a minute. "I've heard some kids and volunteers talking. You are really grabbing their attention."

Her words wound their way around his core. Yes, he enjoyed preparing the Bible lessons, but her encouraging words captivated him. He lobbed a red bag, and it completely missed the board.

He snuck a glance at Brenna, and she had her head cocked to the side. "You okay there, champ?"

What he spotted on her features took him back to high school. But they weren't together anymore.

She'd grown into an even more gorgeous woman these past ten years. He focused on the remaining bags in his grasp. Was he starting to care for her again?

He shook away the unwelcome realization and focused on the Bible lessons. He proceeded to tell her all about his week teaching the kids.

"Probably the biggest thing I learned in preparing for the lessons is that I haven't kept God first." His heart pricked as he said the truth out loud. He felt bad about falling away from the most important relationship in his life. He had been relying on self. But these past few weeks, his relationship with God had reignited and Owen was praying about the next steps for his career.

"Well, you've had a lot going on," Brenna stated. He didn't correct her. He didn't want her to know that for some reason, he'd been a little aloof toward God since high school. He pushed the thoughts to the back burner to analyze at a later date.

"So, tell me more about the youth ministry you volunteered with back in North Carolina," she asked.

He told her all about his duties. "Also, Willow and I were in the middle of starting a youth program at our local community center." He heard the longing in his voice. Even though it would never happen, the dream had been on his heart lately.

She threw her hand to her chest, covering her heart. "Owen, that is so admirable. I wonder if you could do something like that here?"

Maybe. But as a single father, he wasn't sure how much, if any, spare time he'd have.

He and Brenna collected their cornhole bags and agreed to the best out of three. He settled behind the board and lobbed a bag, sinking it into the hole.

Two weeks of working together had already begun to heal the wound Brenna had left when she ghosted him. Sure, he'd like to know why, but he'd pushed it into the past and tried to move on. Thankfully, they were getting along so well that he wondered why they had broken up. He opened his mouth to ask but then spotted Lulu staring at him. As though she could read his mind and didn't want Owen to raise the topic. When he had tried to bring up the blocked calls the other day, Brenna had been adamant about not wanting to discuss their past. Since they had reconnected so well as friends, he decided to respect her wishes.

She sank another blue bag and danced around again. Lulu stood and thrust the tennis ball at Brenna's feet. Brenna picked it up and tossed it. Lulu went flying after it. Right now, Brenna seemed carefree and confident, but Owen knew better.

Now that he knew about the home invasion, he felt an overwhelming desire to protect her. Their gazes locked, and she smiled. His pulse quickened at her attention. For some reason, the knowledge of her difficult past drew her to him like a moth to the flame.

Had he never stopped caring for her? He pushed his possible attraction aside to deal with later. Much later.

The possibility scared him more than being

thrown off a high-strung gelding onto the hard ground below.

He'd have to be careful, because he didn't want to risk having his heart broken again. And the reason for Brenna leaving would always hang over them as long as she kept it a secret.

Chapter Eight

The following Friday, the last car left the afternoon pickup with gravel dust swirling behind. Brenna held up her hand and he high-fived her. Her grin was contagious, and it didn't take long for Owen to forget the troublemakers he'd had today as he slapped her hand and looked forward to a relaxing weekend. Lulu gave them an excited bark and circled around her owner as though wanting to join in.

"This marks the halfway point," she said, sporting a casual outfit, unlike the clothing she wore a few weeks ago. She no longer looked like she wanted to hide. A gentle breeze brushed escaped wisps from her messy ponytail against her cheek. Even though volunteers milled about, his gaze mingled with Brenna's and the warm look she gave him zinged into his chest. Whoa, what was that? His eyes widened and he took a step away. He shook off what he feared might be attraction. He'd only been without Willow for a few months. Well, five, but this interest in his high-school flame still seemed wrong. He didn't want to sully Willow's memory.

Their afternoon volunteers, led by Hazel Murray, scurried off to the stables to start the cleanup process. For some reason, he and Brenna seemed content remaining in the shade of the pavilion.

Brenna removed Lulu's vest and ruffled her fur. "Are you as excited as we are, girl?" The dog lowered the front half of her body to the ground in a playful stance, then zoomed around the pavilion. She was apparently just as happy as they were that they'd made it to the halfway mark and a free weekend was before them.

Except the excitement within Owen quickly morphed into worry. Three more weeks left of camp. The uncertainty about what he'd do with his life continued to gnaw at him. He was a widower with an infant and no feasible job or home. Five months ago, he was working at a job he loved, was married to the love of his life, and had a bright future. That car accident had stolen his wife and changed everything. Had turned his life and expectations upside down.

Brenna picked up a fuzzy tennis ball and threw it into the field beyond the pavilion. Lulu chased after it, returning with the ball and a grin. Evie, sitting in the front carrier on Owen's chest, kicked her feet. He ruffled her hair. She loved facing outward these days so she could see the action. Since his mother had a medical appointment, he'd relieved her of her duties right before the afternoon pickup began and strapped Evie into the carrier.

"Why is it that dogs have such a deep, unconditional love?" Brenna asked, her voice full of wonder. "I mean, no matter how I act toward Lulu, whether I'm having a bad day or whatever, she's always by my side." Her attention switched to Evie, and she tickled the girl under her chin. As close as she was standing, he could smell the sunscreen Brenna probably applied before the afternoon campers arrived. "I guess that's how you feel toward Evie."

Even though worry about his future career churned in his gut, he smiled at his baby. "Absolutely. I can't imagine her ever doing something to make that natural feeling go away."

"But it isn't an automatic thing, because my parents never loved me like that." She tossed the ball again. "Of course, your parents are different. They obviously love all of you unconditionally."

She was right. His parents had raced to the hospital after Willow's accident without a second thought of the rift between them. The ten years of awkwardness lay at his feet, not theirs. They'd reached out to him, but he chose to ignore their attempts. The tension that had developed between him and his parents was all his fault. He knew it. Yet, during that time, his parents had unconditionally loved him.

The other day, his mother had told him they'd not been disappointed, just concerned he hadn't thought through his sudden life choices. Now that Owen was a parent, he got it.

He couldn't imagine Evie making a huge decision without consulting with him first. He shuddered at the speculation. Raising his daughter alone was daunting. Sure, his parents and siblings were around, but he missed having a partner to share the responsibilities, and joys, with.

"Oomph." Brenna threw the ball again. "I hope I don't get tennis elbow from this." Her low laugh captivated him, stirring up memories from the past that he desperately didn't want to remember.

She glowed. Lulu returned, dropped the toy in her dish and slurped up some water. Then the dog snatched her ball and collapsed in a heap, panting and grinning away.

Right now, Brenna was so carefree, like back in high school. Co-leading camp was good for her. He was thrilled at her increased confidence these days. For some reason, he really cared about her emotional growth. Was it because he knew the details of the horrible situation she'd endured or something more?

She caught his gaze and giggled at her dog.

Her expression slammed into him and got his heart pounding. Could she hear it above Lulu's panting? He tried to tamp down his growing emotions toward her. Were old feelings rising up again? Maybe because they'd always shared a special connection? He wasn't sure, but they weren't welcome.

Brenna grabbed a wide contractor broom and began sweeping, collecting the paper water cups the campers had discarded. He took the matching blue bristle broom and followed at a slower pace because Evie kept reaching for the handle.

Lulu waited on the edge of the concrete and as soon as Brenna neared, she pushed her ball at her owner, who picked it up and tossed it across the yard. Evie squealed and kicked her legs. His daughter's excitement reminded him of his commitment to Willow. Brenna was his past, certainly not his future.

Brenna turned and reached out to touch Evie's arm. "She has grown up so much in the past month. I've never really been around children this much, so this has been amazing to see." The way she directed such love and compassion toward Evie wound its way around Owen's heart. Was it possible to love again?

No, he roughed a hand over his face. It wouldn't be right, would it?

What if he surrendered to the temptation and

gave him and Brenna a second shot? Was she was even interested? He wasn't sure. He'd never thought he'd care about another woman again, but then Brenna had stepped back into his life.

After Lulu caught the ball, she must have had a lot of momentum because she did a somersault and landed on her feet, only to race back toward them.

Evie squealed again. He and Brenna exchanged an amused look. Then his gaze drifted to her ruby lips and he wondered, what if?

No. Oh no. He could not be drawn to Brenna's kissable lips.

He took a step back. He'd have to be careful so they wouldn't accidentally fall back into caring for one another like they had in high school.

Hazel Murray, their main afternoon volunteer, shuffled over. Owen was grateful for the interruption. "Other than moving the picnic tables, I think we're done picking up," she said. "Do you need anything else before we all take off?"

Before he could answer her, the crunch of tires over gravel sounded and they all turned. A police car had pulled into the parking area. Brenna sucked in a breath and Lulu raced to her side. Even without the emotional support vest on, the mini Bernedoodle paid attention to Brenna's reactions.

The sight of something Brenna might be

scared of chased away any notion of a romance between them. They were friends. And he wanted the best for his friend.

Brenna reached down to touch Lulu and her chin lifted in an *I can handle this* way.

Instead of rushing over to the cruiser, he walked beside Brenna, allowing her to digest a police car in their parking lot and what it could mean.

Though it was likely a friendly call, he could only imagine what Brenna's imagination was conjuring up.

"What can I help you with?" she asked the officer without a tremble in her voice. Owen was proud that she'd spoken to a strange man without a hand on her dog for emotional support.

"I'm here to speak with Owen," the officer said with a smile on his lips. He introduced himself as the chief of police, then proceeded to tell Owen that he'd heard he was back in town and was relocating here. Then Chief Barker offered him an officer position in the Serenity Police Department.

Owen was floored. Not that he wanted to return to police work, but maybe this was part of God's plan?

Brenna cleared her throat and then turned to walk away. Well, stalk away.

What was going on with her? Didn't she understand he wasn't interested in returning to law enforcement work? Or maybe he was. He turned his full attention to the chief.

He asked Chief Barker a couple of questions about the position and then told him that he'd have to pray about it. After the chief gave Evie some attention, he left.

As Owen returned to the pavilion, waving at the volunteers who drove from the parking area one by one, he was in shock over the unsolicited job offer. Had it conveniently landed in his lap for a reason? He didn't think so because his stomach churned in turmoil over the thought of returning to police work.

That evening, after he put Evie to bed, he immersed himself in preparing for the next few Bible lessons, but the job offer kept spinning around in his mind. Or, more importantly, the lack of a future plan.

He couldn't live with his parents forever, but he'd learned one thing today—he was at peace with his decision to stay in or around Serenity. He'd missed so much by cutting himself off from his family. He wanted to make up for lost time. His wife had been right about having their daughter grow up around relatives. And thankfully Willow's parents had already given him their blessing to move back to Texas.

But other than law enforcement, what other

career would satisfy him and pay about the same? He had no idea.

Was this sudden job offer God's way of providing?

If so, why did Owen's gut roil at the thought of returning to police work?

As soon as Chief Barker extended the job offer to Owen, Brenna rushed to her apartment and turned the oven on. She didn't have a plan, but knew that baking would calm her. Lulu settled in her cozy bed.

Owen had declared he was not looking for a police job. His statement had ignited a glimmer of hope that they could have a future. She'd never make him choose between her and his career. Now law enforcement was back on the playing field. Tears threatened, but she forced them to dry.

She had seen the longing in his eyes at Chief Barker's offer. Why had Owen hidden his wish to work in law enforcement? Leaning against the kitchen island, she felt her tense muscles quivering. She pushed away the anger and plugged her mixer in, gathering the ingredients she'd need.

Why was she even considering the possibility of a future with anyone? Based on what happened six months ago, she just wanted to get back to a normal life. And she didn't think a relationship with a man was in her future. Not with that particular wound.

Now, four hours later, there were dozens of pumpkin chocolate chip muffins, snickerdoodle cookies and another batch of half-moon cookies, a fan favorite, scattered over the smallish island and the folding table she'd purchased to hold baked goods. What in the world was she going to do with all these treats? She washed and dried her hands as inspiration hit. Tomorrow afternoon, she'd deliver goodies to her hardworking volunteers. They'd appreciate a sweet treat over the weekend and if she didn't get them out of the house, she'd eat them. And these days, her weight was one of the few things she felt she could control.

Early the following morning, she let herself into the Confectionery Bakery kitchen. The smell of sweet goodness greeted her.

"Good morning," Edith sang out while she poured a bag of sugar into a commercial mixer.

Usually, arriving here brought Brenna a sense of calm. There was something about baking or the ingredients she used that soothed her. But today, after staying up late and tossing and turning over the job offer Owen had received from the police chief, she felt troubled. She wanted Lulu by her side, but this was a bakery where they prepared food for customers. It would be selfish of Brenna to bring her dog here, even though she had every legal right to.

She hung her purse by the door and slipped on a black apron, scanning the items on the cooling rack.

"You must have gotten here earlier than usual," she said over the noise of the mixer.

Edith turned off the mixer and swiped at her brow. "I woke up before my alarm went off, so I figured I'd come down." She lived above the bakery. Seemed her life was this place. And Brenna envied the woman for having such a clear purpose in life.

"Are you okay? You look exhausted." The older woman crossed the room and put her palm on Brenna's forehead. "Sit. I'll get us a cup of java and we can chat." She scurried over to the industrial coffeepot and poured two steaming mugs while Brenna sank into a seat. "I'm ahead of schedule, so tell me what's going on." She pierced Brenna with the knowing look of a woman who had lost her husband to an illness and struggled to repair a fractured relationship with two of her children. The baker had been through the wringer.

"He lied to me," Brenna said after sharing what had happened with the police chief's arrival yesterday. Edith knew everything else. Why not share the latest news? Her chest ached that Owen didn't feel he could be truthful with her.

"If Chief Barker came calling unannounced, maybe Owen didn't know anything about it?"

"You should have seen how his eyes lit up at the offer." Though, right before the police car arrived, when he'd focused on her lips, she wondered if he was about to lean down and kiss her. But now she was mad at him, angry even. She didn't want to remember that exciting moment that was burned into her memory.

"I know you're worried because of what happened with your father, but what are the chances Owen would get caught in gun fire in Serenity?"

Hmm. She hadn't thought of it that way. Maybe... Her eyes widened.

"No," Brenna stated. "What am I thinking? After the assault. I don't know, trusting someone as a friend has been hard. But getting involved with someone romantically?" Vehemently, she shook her head. "I can't see that happening. With anyone." Edith gave her a knowing look.

"I understand," her friend said. "You were probably scared when the police cruiser arrived like that."

Her eyebrows scrunched together as she tried to bring the moment to mind. So much had happened since then that she'd not really reflected on the cruiser's arrival with a strange man at the helm. "Actually, I didn't. In fact, Lulu didn't nudge me until the chief laid out his offer."

"Oh, Brenna, how exciting." She gave a little clap. "Sounds like maybe you are making a breakthrough."

Brenna thought back over the week and realized the interaction with the parents had been going well. Even that additional altercation with Mrs. Hudson hadn't left her the least bit sweaty. She smiled at the baker as hope for her future bloomed. "Maybe."

"Have you gone to your parents yet to clear the air?" Her excited feeling gave way to trepidation. Brenna wasn't sure she had the emotional energy to deal with her parents. Ever. But her counselor had recommended doing just that. And Edith was her cheerleader.

"No. Not yet."

"You are stronger than you realize. I bet you can handle them." Brenna nodded at her friend but wondered if spending time with her parents would cause her to regress.

"We'll see." She didn't want to make an empty promise.

"Okay, we have like two more minutes. I want to hear about playing cornhole with Owen. We got interrupted last week, and that sounded like a story I wanted to hear."

Her cheeks flamed at the memory. She spilled

all about the evening, especially about how playing cornhole with Owen had felt so normal. As had their high five yesterday afternoon and then the almost-kiss before the police cruiser arrived. "Anyway, regardless of what happens, or doesn't happen, with Owen, I am starting to feel more and more normal with each passing day." And for that, she could thank her counselor and Cora for pushing her to co-lead camp. Something she had originally fought taking on.

Edith stood and gave her a hug. "I'm so happy for you, Brenna. You've worked hard to get here. Now let's go bake!"

The older woman walked over to the mixer and began spooning out the batter for cookies. Before Brenna could help, her phone dinged with a text.

"Take that before your hands get messy," Edith said.

The message was from Emma, Owen's sister-in-law.

My baker had a kitchen fire this morning! Can I buy something, anything, from the bakery at a wholesale price? If I knew ahead of time, I would have asked you to bake for my store at your apartment (your stuff is always so yummy), but I didn't know I'd need fresh baked goods today. Hoping you can help.

A vision of the delectable baked goods overflowing her kitchen island and folding table floated through Brenna's mind. Her thumbs hovered over the keyboard, wondering if the patrons of Emma's family store would like her sweets. Should she put herself out there? Maybe she should just ask Edith if she had any spare baked goods. Surely she could provide for Emma's needs. Brenna nibbled her bottom lip in indecision. Before she could second-guess herself anymore, she typed.

I have fresh pumpkin chocolate chip muffins, snickerdoodles and half-moon cookies on my kitchen counter (I went on a baking binge last night). I can bring over whatever you want.

Since Emma had promised an entire cake for the ladies' tea at church this afternoon, she said she'd take the whole lot. Brenna's phone dinged with a text. She wiped her hands and saw a reply from Emma, and was thrilled at the price her friend was offering. Apparently Brenna was getting the amount a professional baker received. Though baking was an expensive hobby, this figure paid for the ingredients as well as a nice sum for her time. She did a little happy dance and then pocketed her phone.

"What's going on?" her dear friend and mentor asked. She told her about Emma's need and the baking she had done the night before. Edith grinned and congratulated her.

She joined Edith and started spooning out batter onto commercial cookie sheets while she waited for her heartbeat to return to normal.

The sale of her baked goods brought her out of the funk of contemplating a possible relationship with Owen, not that she could get involved with anyone again, even if he was interested. That simply didn't seem possible. Maybe it was providential that she'd been there yesterday to hear the job offer in person. Because it had slammed her back to reality.

Though she had loved Owen ten years ago, her fear over his chosen profession had won over.

And now she held a new fear that was driving her life.

Except, the way he'd looked at her lips yesterday had made her heart flip, even today. The man still took her breath away. Had he been about to kiss her before they'd been interrupted? She shook her head.

No. Owen had just lost the love of his life and Brenna was in no condition to have a romantic relationship.

As much as her feelings for Owen were returning, the safest route for everyone involved was to remain friends.

No matter how much she cared for Owen, she couldn't see them working. The smartest thing to do was move forward in her life.

Because she didn't believe she had the courage to open her heart to someone again.

Chapter Nine

The next week, Brenna lifted a cupcake for all to see, shooting a glare at the giggling girls in the back as she demonstrated an intricate swirl to the teens. The trio were distracting not only her, but some of the other campers. But instead of highlighting the ruckus in the back of the room, Brenna focused on the excitement building in the classroom along with the sweet smell of the fresh cupcakes they were icing.

"Girls," she raised her voice a tad to get their attention. Since it was the fourth week of camp, they should know better. For a moment, they straightened, but it didn't take long for them to huddle and start whispering again. When Lulu heard her owner's voice raised, she got up from her bed and sat at attention beside Brenna in case she was needed.

Brenna blew out an exasperated breath, making stray strands of hair tickle her face as they slipped from her messy ponytail. She had dubbed the trio in the back *the mean girls*, because she had heard them gossiping about what others were wearing in a disparaging manner. They also seemed to look down their noses at others, especially the younger ones that appeared to idolize them.

Brenna had spoken with other volunteers and they were also having difficulty engaging with these girls. In a way, Brenna was happy to hear the feedback because she was concerned they weren't interested in baking and decorating, or perhaps Brenna wasn't doing a very good job teaching. But apparently these girls were only interested in chatting.

As camp co-leader and class teacher, she needed to nip this behavior in the bud. But how?

All of a sudden, she heard a strange noise. Like a scratching. Her gaze moved from the window to the door, where she spotted Owen leaning against the frame. The Victory Youth Camp logo stretched across his chest quite nicely. Her pulse quickened at the sight of him. But she had campers waiting for instruction, so she focused on them and finished her tutorial on how to hold the piping bag at an angle.

While the teens were glued to her detailed piping display, seemingly impressed with her skills, Lulu headed back to her bed.

"I've only seen that on YouTube," someone muttered, awe clinging to their tone. That made

Brenna feel good. Accomplished. Except half of the class's attention was on the noisy girls.

Something in the back of the room glinted, and she spotted a cell phone. She put the cupcake down and made a beeline to the back of the class and the three teens distracting all of them. She held out her hand.

"Phone," she stated with a frown. All campers were required to deposit their devices in a color-coded basket upon arrival. The phones were given back when they returned to the pavilion during closing time. How dare these girls think they didn't have to follow the rules like everyone else did.

The blonde, who seemed like the leader, handed her phone over. Before Brenna withdrew her hand, the other two added theirs. Huh. She had no idea they'd all had their phones. The three girls sneered at her, but there was only about an hour left today.

"These cupcakes are going to the nursing home tonight," Brenna stated as she returned to her spot at the front of the class. "So they are extra special, as some residents don't have loved ones visiting every day. Let's get started." The girls in the back just ignored her and kept talking. Fine. Now that the instructions were over, their chatting was no longer disruptive.

Except, for some reason, what the girls thought

of her mattered to Brenna. She hated that about herself, but the opinion of others did affect her. She ignored the girls and focused on the campers who wanted to be in the class, noticing Owen was no longer standing in the doorway to take her breath away.

A girl raised her hand and Brenna went over to help. She asked Brenna to design a heart on the top of the white frosting in red. Aw, sweet. She complied, and those five completed cupcakes looked gorgeous. "Good job." She patted the teen on the back, and the girl looked up at her and smiled. She basked in the light of the girl's thankful expression, which reminded her how much she had enjoyed teaching third grade before the break-in and assault. Would she ever get back to normal? And when would she figure out what she wanted to do with her life if she didn't return to teaching? She hated the indecision almost as much as her current weakness.

As she was walking away, she heard the mean girls making fun of a cupcake. She turned around and spotted one of the younger girls with a cupcake in front of her that was about to topple over from the amount of frosting she'd layered over it. Brenna went over and expertly removed the top half of the frosting and recommended a way to fix the decoration to cover up the blunder.

"Thank you." The girl hugged her and Brenna

eyed the mean girls over the top of the little girl's ponytail as she made a decision.

She straightened and made herself as tall as possible before she joined the three girls in the back of the room.

"That was mean," she said, making sure to keep her voice low enough so only they'd hear her. Her heart started racing at addressing this conflict. She hoped the girls wouldn't notice her entire body shaking with nervousness. "All three of you will apologize to Katie for that cruel comment. And after camp, you will join me and Mr. Owen when we deliver the baked goods to the nursing home. I want you to see firsthand how much these yummy creations, no matter what they look like, mean to the elderly." They started complaining, but Brenna put up her hand. "I will contact your parents to let them know what happened today and that it wasn't an isolated incident. I'll have them meet us at the nursing home at six to pick you up."

She lifted her chin and roamed the class, trying to stop her body from shaking. She helped those that asked and praised everyone. By the time she made it through the classroom, the shaking had ended.

What would Owen think of these three girls tagging along this afternoon? She didn't really care, because the girls deserved a punishment.

And frankly, delivering cupcakes was far from a punishment. But maybe, just maybe, when they spotted the glee on the residents' faces, they'd feel some compassion.

Except, she had been looking forward to spending some quality time with Owen. But maybe it was better if the two of them had a distraction. Because she didn't need to be teased with even a sliver of hope, as there was no future for them as a couple.

Soon enough, the class ended and the teens rotated into another class. Since she and Owen kept their first and last rotation free to deal with camp stuff, she went to the office and settled in the rolling chair. Lulu got comfortable in her bed while Brenna wiped her sweaty palms on her shorts, nervous about calling the parents of the three girls. She hoped they would be on board.

She called each of them and explained about the disruption and asked for permission to bring the girls with them when she and Owen dropped off the goodies at the nursing home. The first two parents gave the green light for the excursion and agreed to pick their children up there.

The third call was odd because Isabella's mother seemed almost happy to not have the teen for a few hours. Brenna pressed the red button on her phone, approvals complete.

"I did it," she told Lulu, who had been intently

watching her. Her dog rushed over for a pet and then raced to the corner for her ball.

She chuckled. Was Lulu giving her the ball as a prize for handling the situation all by herself, without needing her emotional support dog?

She smiled as excitement fluttered in her belly. Maybe she truly was healing.

Maybe she could get back to her former self someday soon.

Later that afternoon, teens streamed into the pavilion for a Word from God. They were laughing and poking and prodding one another while they chatted. What a change from the first few days when some of the campers didn't know anyone and appeared like outcasts. In the first week, one of the volunteer's jobs was to identify the uncomfortable kids who didn't belong to a group and assimilate them. It appeared they'd been successful.

"Hey, Mr. Owen," Timmy said as he walked by with a couple of buddies, a smile on his face. Owen greeted the boy with a handshake and a pat on the back. He'd been sprinkling lessons about how to greet others properly into the horseback riding sessions with the afternoon campers. He grinned. They were simple things that brought a confident change in these young men's postures and features.

He shook hands with a number of other teens as they streamed in. He had enjoyed building a relationship with the youth, specifically the afternoon group of older kids, and he'd miss them when camp ended.

"These boys look up to you," Hazel said from beside him. "I don't know if it's because you have a military and law enforcement background or you preach amazing sermons—"

"I don't preach," he interrupted his staff volunteer. "And they aren't sermons. They are Bible lessons." He loved preparing them because he'd grown so much closer to the Lord in his studies. And he'd finally grown comfortable standing in front of the morning and afternoon campers, teaching them what God had taught him.

Hazel gave him a knowing smirk and went over to address a group of arguing girls. Before he could figure out what her facial expression meant, movement from the office area captured his attention. His gaze connected with Brenna, and a vibration hummed between them that startled him. He longed to flee his confusing feelings but stood rooted in place. Since he was about to give his Bible teaching, he couldn't leave. He shook off the sudden and unexpected attraction and moved closer to the podium in preparation to speak.

He had become used to speaking in front

of the kids and the volunteers and especially Brenna. Like a personal cheerleader, she was there every day, with supportive nods.

His father stepped beside Brenna and gave her a casual side hug. What was his father doing here? He palmed the back of his neck. *Lord, don't let me mess up while my father is watching.* Then his mother arrived. Owen's eyes widened as she hobbled over on crutches. She hugged Brenna like she hadn't seen her in days when he knew for a fact they'd shared a quick cup of coffee before camp this morning.

As the kids found their seats, his mother took his father's hand and gave Owen a reassuring smile, but it only made his palms sweatier. With his parents here, he felt like he was on stage, being watched. Were they observing him as a test? Did they feel like he couldn't handle this part of camp? He shook off the negative thoughts and focused on the outline of his Bible lesson.

He stepped behind the podium, where he'd neatly laid his notes earlier. Today, he planned to talk about leaning on God. Since this was such a large topic, he'd made it his series for the entire week.

Making eye contact with each child, he shared what God had taught him over the weekend, rarely glancing at his notes. Early on, he'd learned the more he focused on his notes, the less engaged the campers were. So he'd worked to internalize the message. He taught from a couple of bullet points, giving as many real-life examples as possible.

When he finished the lesson, he said a prayer for the remainder of their day and released them to their next session.

As the kids erupted in noise and shuffled off to their next rotation, he glanced at his father, who looked introspective. Or maybe disappointed, Owen couldn't tell. But he didn't appear proud at all. Yet what did Owen expect after he'd minimized communication between them for years? He took a step toward his father, hoping to hear some positive feedback, but noticed Timmy and his friends lingering, as though they had an urge to talk with him.

After the lesson about relying on God, Owen wanted to hear what was on the boys' hearts, assuming they were willing to share. On the other hand, he was curious about his father's thoughts, too. But his job, and the right thing to do, won out.

"Are you boys having a good afternoon?" D.J. and Timmy nodded, but Zeke dug the toe of his sneaker into the concrete below.

Owen moved to a nearby picnic table and motioned the boys to follow. He always liked to talk with children at their level. With the morning campers, he crouched down. But with the older kids, he found that sitting put them at ease.

Zeke started off, telling Owen about issues he'd been having with his father. D.J. and Timmy nodded along, like they already knew about the problems. One of Owen's examples had lit a fire under Zeke—he knew he needed to rely on God during this trial. Owen's heart was full that his teaching had prompted the boy to come to this earnest conclusion.

After the discussion was over, Owen prayed for all three boys. Zeke lifted his face and met Owen's gaze. "Thank you." Owen blinked back the sudden emotion at how much the teen had grown over the past few weeks. Was this how parents felt as their children matured? Boy, did Owen have a journey with Evie in front of him.

When the boys departed, he sidled up to his parents.

"We are so proud of you, Owen," his father stated, swiping the back of his hand along his cheek. Was he teary-eyed? Owen wanted to beam in excitement over his father's praise, but he kept a neutral face. "Since you opened your mouth thirty minutes ago, and I saw how you captured the teens' attention and I spotted the passion in your eyes, I've been wondering if you could parlay these skills into a new career," his father said. "But I don't know what."

He shrugged. Huh. Owen had never considered doing whatever this was for a living. Wasn't sure it was possible.

"I need to get back," his mother jumped in, "because Laney's watching Evie for me, but I agree with your father, honey. You are doing a wonderful job." Laney, Ethan's wife, was sweet to offer. Before his mother turned, Owen spotted moisture in her eyes as well. He held in an ecstatic whoop at their positive reaction to his teaching. She hobbled away on her crutches, his father beside her.

Based on his parents' positive reaction, was he on track to fully reconciling with them?

"The message was great today. As always." Brenna touched his arm to get his attention. Her soft skin against his gave him a jolt of awareness. He wasn't sure how to feel about his reaction.

"Thanks." He gazed into her face. Her encouragement and warm touch reminded him of their almost-kiss the other day. If they hadn't been interrupted, would he have actually gone through with it and kissed her? He scrubbed a hand over his face. This whole relationship felt unwise.

He shouldn't worry, though, because nothing would happen between them. There was no way he'd fall in love again.

"Don't forget, we are going to the nursing

home after camp ends today." Brenna smiled with her reminder, as though she hadn't upended his whole world with her electrifying touch and mesmerizing smile. She rushed off to the baking room before he could reply.

Why had he agreed to drive her to the nursing home? She was capable of going alone. Or she could get someone else to help. Why him? The last thing the two of them needed was to spend even more time together. Alone.

Then it hit him. Had he never gotten over her?

The moments they'd shared, along with the words they'd exchanged, tumbled through his mind like a movie. A romance movie.

He wanted to smack his forehead because he was right. He still had feelings for her.

Even though he never wanted to move on from Willow, his heart seemed to have another idea.

And he didn't like it at all.

After afternoon pickup, the "mean girls" were under the pavilion, grouped close together at a picnic table. They whispered and shot daggers at Brenna. Why had she given them a consequence? She should have just confiscated their phones and called it a day like any other volunteer would do. But she wasn't just a volunteer. She was a co-leader. And that position came with responsibilities.

"I see we're taking Autumn's minivan," Owen said as he secured the car seat base in the second row of his sister's vehicle. Evie was fussing in the infant car seat that he'd set on the ground.

"I'm sorry." She glanced over her shoulder at the girls, not looking forward to the drive to the nursing home. At least she'd have Owen by her side. "So, you see—"

"Hazel told me what happened." He touched her arm. "I'm proud of you," he whispered. She could feel his breath against her skin and she reveled in the moment. Then he stepped back and gave her a wink, which sent her tummy doing backflips. For the fiftieth time today, she wondered if she could give in and allow this budding romance to grow. She wasn't sure, and she was shocked to find she was even contemplating it. The idea of trusting Owen seemed easier than trusting someone she hadn't known before the home invasion.

Or maybe he just considered her a friend? Well, honestly, the safe route was to stay in the friend zone. She pursed her lips. It was all so confusing.

She patted Lulu, who sat beside her. If he was proud of her for handing out consequences, he'd be thrilled to hear she had done all of it without Lulu's help. But she'd have to wait until later to tell him.

Right as Owen picked up the carrier, Evie went from fussing to bawling. He unstrapped her and placed her on his shoulder, but the crying grew. He started bouncing.

"Maybe I should stay back," he said over her wails.

Brenna sucked in a surprised breath as the girls strolled over to the van.

"Are we leaving soon?" Isabella, the blonde leader, complained.

Brenna could barely breathe at the thought of handling this situation alone. Why had she forced them to visit the nursing home with her? Was it too late to cancel and have their parents come here to pick them up instead? Lulu pressed against her leg and gave a tiny whine.

When Lulu made the noise, Owen's face went from sad to concerned.

Brenna felt so helpless as the start of a panic attack seized her. It had been weeks since she'd had one.

Owen held Evie out and flew her around in a figure eight. It didn't take long for her cries to turn into squeals.

"Okay, girls, into the very back row. We need to get going before Evie gets upset again." The girls loaded in and she gestured with a shaky hand for Lulu to get in the back. Trembling, Brenna settled in the passenger seat, hoping

Owen couldn't see her heart thumping in her chest. Thankful the panic attack hadn't been full blown, she released a relieved breath and tightened her grip on the commercial-size baking sheet nestled in her arms, covered with the treats the campers had created.

Owen loaded Evie into the car seat, then propped up a bottle for her to drink. Shockingly, Isabella crawled to the second row and offered to hold the bottle in place while they drove.

Well, that was a step in the right direction. It didn't take long to get to the nursing home and unload. Evie was happier in Owen's arms rather than the carrier, so he left the car seat in the van. Lulu walked beside the group, her emotional support vest on display.

Brenna stepped up to the receptionist and introduced the woman to the girls. She looked between the girls and Brenna, then stated, "We weren't expecting the teens. I think you were supposed to get approval."

Brenna was at a loss for words. She propped the baking sheet on the counter and worried her lower lip. She was responsible for the girls. What would she do with them while she handed out the cupcakes to the seniors? They couldn't hang out in the parking lot. Anyway, if the girls weren't allowed in, then they wouldn't see how happy the residents were with their "works of art."

Stella, the supervisor, sidled up to the desk and welcomed the girls. She gave Brenna a broad grin and told her to sign the teens in.

"I'm happy to have them here," Stella said. "The more the merrier. Isabella, right?" She gave the girl a hug. "Your mother is my Bible study leader. Brenna, the cupcakes look yummy. The residents will be so thankful."

Isabella's friends twittered behind their hands, but after Stella released her, Isabella took a step away from her friends, which floored Brenna.

"Isabella, could you hold this for me while I sign us in?" The girl's face lit up. She took hold of the tray like her life depended on keeping the sweet treats upright.

"I remember how cute you two looked in high school," Stella stated while Brenna signed them in, her gaze bouncing between Brenna and Owen. "I'm glad to see you back together."

Brenna glanced at Owen, who discreetly shook his head. He was right. There were too many people and too much commotion to straighten out Stella's mistaken impression of them. But as she finished signing the group in, Stella's comment rang out in her head. Brenna had been trying to put him in her rearview mirror, but he was always around. Even though she knew they couldn't have a romantic relationship, their constant togetherness kept reminding her of what she couldn't have.

When she took the tray from the girl, Isabella gave her a look of curiosity. Maybe Brenna could get through to the teen after all. Once Isabella saw how the residents reacted to these cupcakes, surely she'd have more enthusiasm for decorating baked goods in the future, and for the residents who didn't have a family member visit regularly.

Brenna spotted a resident she'd met last week and lifted a hand to wave. But that left the platter of baked goods unsteady. The tray started to wobble, so she halted and tried to get a grip on the edges of the thin baking sheet. But her fingers kept slipping. The whole situation played out in slow motion before her eyes, completely beyond her control.

No! The whole reason the girls were here was to see the reaction on the seniors' faces. She couldn't drop and ruin the cupcakes when they were so close to her goal.

But no matter how she tried, the tray slipped from her fingers and landed with a clatter on the tile floor. She closed her eyes, envisioning the big icing disaster at her feet.

"That was so cool."

"Can you do that again?"

Brenna opened her eyes to discover the baking sheet had landed upright with only a couple of cupcakes tipped over.

Stella rushed over to help clean up the ruined treats while Lulu, proudly wearing her red vest, patiently sat beside Brenna.

"You probably couldn't do that again if you tried," Isabella stated, a smirk in her eyes. But this time, the smirk was more about camaraderie than a mean look. And after weeks of ill behavior, Brenna would take that as a win.

She laughed along with the girls and Owen. Evie even kicked her legs at the scene. Lulu remained seated, but her gaze kept darting to the sweet treats on the floor. But since she was in working mode, she remained on her best behavior even though Brenna knew her dog wanted to scarf up the crushed cupcakes.

When they entered the dining room, a number of seniors came over to exclaim at how creative the cupcakes were. They pointed and laughed and picked their favorites, while Lulu walked over to an elderly man sitting alone and put her chin on his leg. The man's faded eyes lit up as he reached a shaky hand out to pet Lulu.

All three girls' features went from disinterested to excited, as they pointed out the cupcakes that their youngest fellow camper had decorated, as though they were proud of their camp buddy.

Brenna's heart was full. And the teens' parents were going to be thankful for this little field trip, because it looked like a lightbulb had switched on in the girls' demeanor.

Camp was not only helping Brenna heal, but she had gotten herself back into teaching mode with these girls, which she found fulfilling. Except, teaching in a classroom still didn't hold her interest.

She frowned as that familiar gnawing started in her gut again. What was she going to do for a career when camp ended in two weeks?

Chapter Ten

Sunday morning, the praise band played their final notes to close out the church service. Some parishioners stood and rustled about to collect their belongings, while others turned to chat with those around them. Owen remained seated with Evie sound asleep in the crook of his arm.

"We'll see you at the blanket," Owen's mother whispered as she slipped out of the pew and followed the others out the large wooden double doors.

Timmy, D.J. and Zeke stopped to high-five Owen. He awkwardly lifted his left palm to his high school campers, thrilled they'd found each other over the summer. And also pleased to find them in church today. Maybe what Owen had been teaching was taking root in their hearts. "See you out there," he called as they hurried away.

Though Owen wanted to mingle at the monthly potluck on the back lawn, he was a sweaty mess where Evie was lying against him. Going outside would only make both of them hotter, but staying in the church wasn't an option either.

Parents stopped to thank him for his Bible teachings, which embarrassed Owen and got him gathering his things. With his free hand, he collected the half-empty formula bottle and stuck it in the backpack that he now used as a diaper bag.

Laney and her three kids slipped past him as Ethan slid over.

"Going outside?" his brother asked. Owen glanced around, noticing most people had already departed, so there was no rush.

"Maybe in a minute. She's comfortable in the air conditioning. The heat will probably wake her." Though he expected she would startle awake as soon as the sanctuary emptied and became quiet, because that was how his daughter rolled.

"Heard Mom and Dad talking about how great your sermon was the other day."

"It wasn't a sermon, it was a Bible lesson. There's a huge difference."

Ethan nodded. "My point was they were proud of you. Seems like maybe this chasm you talk about has evaporated."

"I hope so." The past couple of days, he'd felt peace. This morning he was able to put a finger on why. "Cutting Mom and Dad out of my life messed up my relationship with God." His mood dampened when Ethan's eyebrows rose. Perhaps his brother was disappointed with Owen, too. "Now that things seem normal between us again, and I've been working on these Bible lessons and spending time with God, I realized that during my time away, I hadn't been keeping God first."

"Today's a new day," Ethan responded. Gracious. And Owen appreciated that. Maybe it hadn't been disappointment on his brother's face earlier.

"I took what Mom and Dad said when I was eighteen and twisted it into something they didn't mean. Then I started living for myself."

"Sometimes the times when we stray from God make us more appreciative of His promises." So true. Owen had been reading the Word with such hunger since camp started.

Evie stirred and Owen looked around. Sure enough, the space was empty and now whisper-quiet. Evie startled awake and gazed into Owen's face. His chest filled with love. Yes, he missed Willow, but Evie was his future. Willow wouldn't want him to stop living because she was gone. Sometime over the past few weeks, he'd come to terms with his wife's death. He'd also stopped blaming himself for the accident.

A creak sounded next to him as Ethan stood. "Well, I should check to see if Laney needs any help with the kiddos. Though her morning sickness is gone, she now gets tired real easy."

"I'm excited for the new baby—another niece to dote on." He smiled at the glee on his brother's face. Even though Owen had been out of the family for years, they'd welcomed him back with open arms. Since his return, he'd been enjoying spending time with his nieces and nephews. "We should get out there, too. Right, Evie?" He propped his five-month-old on his hip and slung the backpack on his free shoulder.

Owen and Ethan skirted through the air-conditioned hallways to the back exit. Ethan opened the door, and the July humidity took Owen's breath away. Tents were set up over long tables to keep the food covered from the blazing sun. People milled about under the tents, going through the buffet line.

Owen spotted Brenna across the way, standing in the shade with Lulu. He felt a pull toward her, but he was with Ethan right now. There had to be two hundred people here, and she was the first one he noticed. Her floral sundress hugged her body as she tossed her head back, likely laughing at some joke. Her renewed confidence had allowed her to resume dressing like her usual self.

"You sure there isn't something going on between you two?" Owen glanced at his brother and realized he'd been caught staring.

"No. Of course not. Willow was my one."

Ethan cocked his head. "But Willow is gone. She wouldn't want you to pine away. Or raise Evie alone, would she?"

No, she wouldn't.

"Remember how Brenna dumped me without even a conversation?" Owen scowled.

"It's been ten years, man." His brother scoffed at him. "Give her a break. You never know what God has planned for you." With those parting words, his brother took off to find his pregnant wife.

What had Owen done to make her block his calls? They had graduated, gone to the parties and bonfire, and then hugged good-night. He thought they had parted on good terms, with Brenna packed and ready to leave in the morning for the elite teacher summer camp she'd been accepted into. And then, with no warning, she'd cut him out of her life.

She had been on his mind for the past ten years. Sure, he'd entered the military and become consumed with his new life and his new girlfriend. He'd fallen in love and married another woman, but there was always a part of him that wondered what in the world had happened.

He weaved through the crowd, with Evie on

his hip. "Did you have a good time with the other kids in Sunday school?" He looked at her and she kicked her feet, which was her favorite activity lately. His mother told him she'd be an early walker. Especially because she had so many cousins running around to watch.

He couldn't get his father's comment about parlaying his Bible teaching skills into some type of job. But the only occupation that came to mind was a schoolteacher. And he wasn't sure he was cut out to teach history. Certainly not literature or math or science.

The Bible teachings and the response he was getting from the boys especially reminded him of the ministry he and his wife had planned. He switched Evie to his other hip. Part of him wished the Bible teaching aspect could be permanent, but Victory Youth Camp wasn't a year-round endeavor.

Hazel Murray, their afternoon volunteer leader, stopped him to coo over his daughter. Evie grinned up at her and kicked her legs. "You are doing an amazing job with the Bible teachings, Owen. Not only are they personal and informative, but the kids are on the edge of their seats when you open the Bible and talk." Heat crawled up his neck, edging toward his cheeks and ears. He quickly thanked her, and they parted ways while he scanned the crowd for Pastor Tony.

His stomach grumbled, but since Evie had taken a bottle during the service, he figured he'd wait on filling a plate until he'd had a chance to talk with Pastor. He hunted him down and waited until he was free.

Pastor Tony turned to him. "The infamous Evie," he said as he touched her bare toes and gave them a tickle. "You looked content drinking a bottle and then sleeping during my sermon." The two men shared a chuckle.

"Don't take it personal, Pastor, she does that to all of us." Owen caught the pastor up on his life, as he hadn't had a chance since he'd arrived back in Serenity. He accepted his pastor's condolences, then told him about the youth program he and Willow had planned to start at a community center in North Carolina, as well as the volunteering he'd done with the youth at his church.

"Are you aware of any opportunities to serve with the youth here in Serenity?" Right then, Evie started crying. She must be hungry since she'd never finished her last bottle. Owen put the backpack on the ground and started rummaging through for the makings of a fresh bottle.

"Can I take her?" With Lulu by her side, Brenna appeared with her arms stretched out. Knowing Evie would calm down in her arms, he handed her over, their fingers mingling during the handoff. Brenna's skin was so soft and feminine, her fingers long and slender. He enjoyed the brief moment, though he probably shouldn't.

Almost as soon as Evie was in Brenna's arms, she calmed down. Brenna spoke in low murmurs to her as he poured a can of liquid formula into a clean bottle and handed it to Brenna.

"In case," he said. She smiled and wove off into the crowd, leaving him with a sense of longing to be by her side. But he shook the errant thoughts away and turned his attention back to Pastor Tony.

Pastor asked for more details on what Owen had done in North Carolina and then told him the church in Love Valley was looking for a youth pastor, and part of his role would be exactly what Owen just described.

"But I'm not a pastor. I just want to volunteer." His pastor didn't respond, but a strange look covered his face as he gave Owen the contact information for Pastor Mark Reed. Owen planned to call as soon as Evie settled for her afternoon nap. Hopefully, the pastor would have a volunteer role for him or God would take away his passion for building into youth. Because what had started out as a seed of interest while Willow was alive had turned intense.

"Give him a call. I'm sure God has big plans for you." What did that mean? A parishioner came up and stole Pastor's attention before Owen could ask him about it.

Come to think of it, his brother had said something similar about Owen and Brenna. *Give her a break. You never know what God has planned for you.*

Maybe Owen had held his grudge against Brenna long enough. They'd practically been kids when she'd ghosted him. Instead of stewing over it, he decided to put the hurt from her blocked calls in the past, where it belonged. The reason probably wasn't even important anymore.

Which begged the question. Could he and Brenna have another chance? Was she even interested in him as more than a friend? Nah. Given the wound from her past, she might not be interested in a relationship with anyone. Ever.

He lifted his chin and scanned the crowd, looking for where his family was camped out. He spotted Brenna's long honey-blond waves swaying around her shoulders as she held Evie happily in her arms, his mother sitting close by.

He released a frustrated breath at his confused thoughts and tunneled his hand through his hair. If he was honest with himself, Brenna captivated him. Maybe more than he'd like to admit.

Now that he'd accepted he wasn't responsible for Willow's accident, it was time to consider moving on with his life.

Was there a chance at a future with Brenna?

Perhaps more importantly, was he ready for another relationship? He shook his head. It felt too soon. Way too soon.

Though it was a hot summer day, there were large industrial fans set up outside the tent blowing on the crowd, keeping the outrageous heat and humidity at bay. While holding Evie in her arms, Cora waved her over and Brenna happily joined the older woman. The McCaws had secured a delightful spot in the canopy of a large oak tree.

Brenna nestled the baby slurping down a bottle against her chest and settled on a soft blanket, her pretty sundress splayed over her legs. Cora and Wade sat in camp chairs and Lulu flopped down beside her. Most of the other McCaw adults chased after their children.

Brenna sighed at how loved and accepted she felt. She was thrilled to be part of the McCaws, at least for the moment. She'd love to be part of a family like this, but her parents were a prime example of what marriage shouldn't be. She found the way they treated each other since the accident alarming. Not that their marriage was great before, but the accident had flipped a switch and turned every interaction into a screaming match. She didn't want that type of drama in her life, so she doubted she'd ever be able to let a man into her life enough to marry him.

Autumn called Lulu over to show her the water dish. Brenna thanked her as Lulu happily drank her fill.

"Evie must be having a growth spurt because she just had a bottle about an hour ago," Cora said, a sparkle in her eyes. She loved being Memaw to her grandchildren. She and Brenna shared a contented look, then Brenna scanned the crowd for her parents. They probably weren't here as they'd given up the pretense of church years ago, but Brenna always liked to know if they were around so she could keep a healthy distance. Her gaze snagged on Owen, who was chatting with Earl Woodward, the town veterinarian.

What had he been talking to Pastor Tony about? It must have been super important because when she took Evie from him, his face held a serious expression. Maybe he was talking to the pastor about Willow? Brenna needed to remember he was still in love with his late wife.

"Aw, she is so cute," Isabella, the afternoon camper, appeared and settled beside Brenna. The teen peered at the baby and Brenna wondered about the girl's sudden appearance. Sure, the nursing home adventure had brought out better behavior in her, but the way she settled on the blanket—as if she actually wanted to be here—surprised Brenna.

As Evie started drinking the second half, Brenna tilted the bottle higher.

"I saw her sleeping in Mr. Owen's arms during the service," Isabella said, cooing over little Evie.

Brenna smiled at the interaction. She'd seen the exchanges between Owen and the older boys, and she wanted that with the afternoon female campers. To create a positive relationship with the girls, like she had herself with the counselors as a teen.

When Evie finished, Brenna stuck the used bottle in the picnic basket. Isabella glanced at Brenna while chewing on her bottom lip. Did the girl want to talk about something? Brenna recalled how distant her mother had sounded when she had called for approval to take the girl to the nursing home. She'd pretty much said "whatever," as though she hadn't cared that her daughter had broken the rules. She almost seemed relieved to have a couple of more hours without the teen.

Brenna made the motion to put Evie on her shoulder to burp, but Isabella extended her hands. "Can I hold her? I babysit, so I know how to burp." Her eyes held so much interest they shone, but Brenna was nervous to relinquish control. Owen had handed the baby over to her, and she wasn't sure what the etiquette was for allowing someone else, especially someone so young, to take over. But she felt like this moment was pivotal in their relationship.

"Sure," she said brightly and settled Evie on the girl's shoulder, the spit-up cloth between them. Beyond Isabella's shoulder, she spotted Owen and her pulse stuttered at how handsome he looked in those khaki pants. The white polo shirt accentuated his dark tan. He caught her eye and gave her a thumbs-up. Her stomach flipped at his sweet gesture. Had he known she'd been nervous about handing Evie over to the teen? He was so sweet to consider her feelings.

The baby burped and Isabella murmured words of encouragement, then laid her on the blanket to let her kick. "She loves to move her arms and legs, doesn't she?" the teen asked.

"She sure does. She's a wiggly baby."

Isabella looked over with a gleam in her eyes. "How long have you and Mr. Owen been dating?"

Brenna sucked in a breath. What? "No." She tried to laugh off the girl's assumption, but a strangled sound came from her throat. "We aren't dating." The last thing she wanted to discuss with a teenager was her feelings toward Owen. She pushed the girl's question away and forced herself to concentrate on Isabella's emotional well-being. Before Brenna lost her nerve, she spoke. "So, how's everything been lately?" It was the only thing she could think of. And it was the question that, as a teen, had usually made her spill her guts.

Isabella didn't look up, but Brenna spotted a hard, visible swallow as her lips pressed tight. Oh no, she shouldn't have said anything. She should have kept her mouth closed.

But then Isabella opened up like a fire hydrant. She spoke quietly about how her parents weren't very involved. How she never did anything right in her mother's eyes. And her father was rarely home, as he was apparently a workaholic.

Brenna's heart fell at what the teen had been dealing with. The people who should love her the most were actually hurting Isabella every day. The story was similar to Brenna's, but just didn't have the on-the-job injury that had put her father in a wheelchair for life. Anxiety churned in her gut. She wasn't sure what to say to Isabella, because the relationship with her own parents had never healed. And she so wanted to let Isabella know she cared and empathized with her.

Lulu stood and slunk over to Brenna. She tried to ignore her emotional support dog, but Lulu groaned and pawed at her owner. Right then, Isabella made eye contact. Brenna was concerned the girl knew she was nervous because of how Lulu was reacting. Evie started squirming, but Brenna didn't want to interrupt the flow of conversation.

Isabella continued to speak about how she wasn't sure her parents loved her. All Brenna could think about was how her own childhood had made her second-guess everything. Even her relationship with Owen. But could she share such personal details with someone she barely knew? Especially a teenager?

"What's my little pumpkin doing?" Owen asked as he leaned down and picked up his squirming baby.

Brenna made eye contact with the girl, something that had been hard for Brenna, but at the moment she felt strong. She told Isabella she got where she was coming from and they'd talk tomorrow. Maybe they could grab coffee or something. The girl's eyes lit up and she eagerly agreed before walking away.

"Sorry. I didn't mean to interrupt." Owen settled beside Brenna, the baby cradled in his arms.

Brenna couldn't get over what Isabella had shared. She'd have to follow up with the teen.

Owen leaned against her as her gaze remained on the teen sauntering away. "I didn't realize you two were having a heart-to-heart." When he straightened and their skin was no longer touching, Brenna missed it. On the other hand, ever since they'd reconnected, Owen had made sure to jump away any time they'd touched. But this time he hadn't. This time he'd lingered.

"You okay?" Owen put his hand on her knee and she gazed into his face. His palm remained as he shot her a sweet smile. The same one he used to give her in high school. Back when they were in love.

In her belly, butterflies took flight, confirming that her feelings for Owen were stronger than ever.

"Hey, I was just talking with Theo from the Morning Grind. He said they have a baking deal with you?"

"Didn't I tell you? They asked if I'd be willing to do a standing order for three rotating baked goods."

"Congratulations." He grinned and moved closer, as though he might engulf her in a hug, but didn't. "Which ones were you thinking about?"

"The blueberry raspberry cream tarts, mini chocolate croissants—"

"Oh, my," he interrupted. "Those croissants you make are delectable." He groaned and licked his lips. She chuckled at his good taste in her baking.

"And they also want those bite-size crinkle

cookies. But I'm not sure about that one, because they want me to have a flavor for every season, a flavor I can't sell to anyone else, and since they want to sell it in sets of three, I'd have to find some type of disposable box, which would cut into my profits."

"Why not wrap them in that clear cellophane and then tie them with a colorful ribbon?"

"I like that. Or I could use cellophane *bags* wrapped with a ribbon." Excitement built in her chest. She could just envision the crinkle cookies in the clear wrapping. And maybe she could use the ribbon to indicate which season the cookie represented.

Chief Barker walked by and greeted them, souring Brenna's mood.

What if Owen took the Serenity police officer's job? Could she emotionally handle it? For the umpteenth time, she turned it around in her mind. Was a small-town cop safer than one in a bigger city? Then a tiny voice inside her head reminded her to trust God.

If Owen wanted a relationship with her, what would she do? What did she want?

The butterflies in her belly swarmed faster.

Without a doubt, she knew she wanted a future with him. She hadn't stopped loving him.

But then the horrid memory of the home invasion and attack assaulted her. Reminding her that the event might keep her from ever being at ease with a man again.

Even Owen.

And her heart ached with that knowledge.

Chapter Eleven

Two weeks later, Owen found himself out to lunch with Brenna on a Saturday afternoon. Well, it wasn't fancy, just Mabel's Diner with old-timey Formica tables and a scratched black-and-white checked floor. He took in the woman across from him, who was wiping away tears from laughing so hard.

"I can't believe he said that." She shook her head in disbelief at a comment from one of their silly afternoon campers. She had matured into a gorgeous woman, with tiny laugh lines around her eyes and lips that made him think she'd led an enjoyable life while they'd been apart.

Why had he asked Brenna to lunch? And in such a date-like setting? Well, not that Mabel's Diner was romantic or anything. But they were alone and eating a meal together. It wasn't like they were teenagers again. Or in a relationship of any kind. He frowned at his foolishness, unsure that having a good time was appropriate.

Evie startled in her car seat sitting on the chair beside him and her eyes popped open. He expertly put together a bottle for her, then settled her in his arms. She sucked with such ferocity that he wondered if his mother was right. Another growth spurt.

"She is so adorable. But you probably get that all the time." Brenna looked at Evie like most women did. Which made him remember that Willow had never gotten a chance to see their baby.

"Yeah. Nobody ever tells me she's adorable," he quipped. His non-date chuckled as Emma, his sister-in-law, stopped by sans triplets.

"Brenna, I just wanted to let you know that my customers are truly enjoying your sweet treats."

"I'm so glad," Brenna said as a blush crept into her cheeks. The color matched the pretty pink top she had on today.

"The baker from Love Valley was amazing, but my customers seem to really like single-serve items. Especially all your yummy baked goods," Emma said as she adjusted the purse strap on her shoulder.

Owen puffed his chest out at the compliment. Why did he feel so proud of his co-leader right now?

"I appreciate the opportunity."

"Brenna, we're like family." Emma's phone

dinged. She pulled it out and read it. "Gotta go. But I just wanted to thank you in person. Even though we only live a few miles apart, I haven't seen you much lately." She gave Brenna a hug and then left.

He lifted Evie to his shoulder and patted her back. "Congratulations. I hadn't heard you were Emma's main baker now."

Brenna's grin widened. "I still can't believe it. And since Edith is close to retiring, this will allow me to keep baking no matter who purchases the bakery."

"I'm so happy for you." He reached across the table to squeeze her hand, and something electric surged through him. He allowed himself to enjoy the moment. She smiled at him, which caused a sudden blip in his pulse. Very strange. "Seems like your dream is coming true."

Before she could answer, their food was delivered. A fragrant burger and fries for him and a green salad with grilled chicken on top for her. He prayed for their meal and then buckled Evie in the wooden high chair.

"That's new," Brenna said.

"Yep. Mom started putting her in the high chair this past week and Evie took right to it." He sanitized the edge of the laminate surface and then pulled her to the edge of the table. "She doesn't even need the towels to support herself anymore." He pulled out a sippy cup full of water and a splash of juice and placed it in front of her. Her eyes lit up, and she reached for the bottle and awkwardly stuffed it into her mouth. She hadn't been drinking from a sippy cup for long now, but it intrigued her. Like the high chair.

"Only one week left," Brenna stated around a small bit of salad. He shoved some crisp fries into his mouth and grinned.

"I think we're going to make it," he declared. They discussed the campers who had struggled at the beginning and how they'd grown in the past five weeks. Owen tried to ignore how much the relationship between him and Brenna had grown as well. During this past month, he'd been able to forgive himself for not driving Willow the day of the accident. And these days, he was willing to admit he was excited about a possible future with Brenna, guilt no longer eating at him for being attracted to someone other than Willow.

"Have you decided what you're going to do after camp? I mean, for a job?" Brenna asked. She glanced down then, her long lashes brushing the tops of her cheeks. When she looked back at him, he got caught in those baby blue eyes with gold flecks swimming in the depths. She was absolutely stunning, especially now that she'd come out of her shell and had stopped fearing her own shadow. Well, at least most of the time.

"I'm not sure." Other than rejecting the police officer's job, he had no idea. A strange look crossed over her face, but he couldn't name the emotion. "How about you?"

"I've ruled out buying the bakery." She made a face. "I don't have the money and frankly it sounds too stressful."

"How about returning to teaching?"

"I don't think I'm ready."

"I think you're handling the parents like a pro." He couldn't get over the transformation he'd seen in her personality. She was now so much like her confident high school self. Except, when she dabbed her lips with a napkin and then put her fork down, he knew from the serious expression on her face that she didn't share his optimism.

"Thank you. I really appreciate the vote of confidence." She took a sip of her ice water. "But I just don't have the passion for teaching like I once did." His eyes widened with surprise. She'd wanted to be a teacher since first grade.

"You do great with the campers."

"You are sweet. But frankly, the thing I enjoy the most is baking. Except I can't make a career out of it." She chuckled. Before he could disagree, Evie started fussing.

She tossed her sippy cup on the floor and then squirmed like she was trying to get out of the high chair. He pulled a teething ring from his backpack and handed it to her. She picked it up and gnawed on it. Yep, teething again. He collected the discarded cup and slipped it into his backpack. When Evie started babbling, Brenna sucked in a breath.

"Is she talking yet?" She seemed enthralled by the "buh" and "puh" sounds Evie was making. "Has she said mommy or daddy yet?"

He stopped chewing at her question, the juicy hamburger turning to sawdust in his mouth. He hadn't thought about when Evie would start to talk instead of babbling nonsense. He and his mother had actively been working with her, but so far she hadn't uttered any real words. When Evie said Mama for the first time, Willow wouldn't be around to hear it. He finished his bite and swallowed, a lump now settling in his throat at the unnerving image. He was not to blame for Willow's accident, but he still felt bad their child would grow up motherless.

Evie's "buh" sounds started to get insistent. So he reached in the middle of the table for a cardboard drink coaster sitting next to a stack of napkins at the same time as Brenna. Their fingers touched and their gazes collided, tangling for a long moment. The connection stirred up a longing to determine if Brenna cared for him as more than a friend.

With shaky hands, he handed the coaster to Evie. She grasped it with glee, turning it around with her chubby fists and sticking the rounded corners into her mouth.

He wasn't sure how it happened, but here they were, baby and all. Almost like a little family. And shockingly having a blast. Why had he asked Brenna out? They weren't in a relationship of any kind, though if he were honest with himself, he'd like to be. Mostly because he'd never stopped caring for her.

And now that he'd come to terms with moving on from Willow, what if he and Brenna could have a relationship? He shook his head. He was a single father now. Would he have time or energy for a relationship?

"How are your meals?" Mabel, the diner owner, asked as she leaned against their table. They both told her everything was superb, as always. "Brenna, your half-moon cookies are so delicious and going over well with my Saturday customers." She crouched down, her white apron bunching up around her neck. She tugged it down. "In fact, I've noticed business surging early on Saturday as everyone tries to get here before I sell out. I was wondering if we could add a couple more days?" Mabel's hopeful look made Owen burst with pride for Brenna. They chatted about the days and amount, Brenna's pretty eyes dancing with excitement. From the payment that they agreed upon, it no longer sounded like baking was a hobby. Brenna might be able to eke out a living with all of these side baking hustles.

As Mabel left, his phone dinged with an incoming text. It was from Evie's new pediatrician, reminding him about her well-baby checkup this week. He groaned.

"What's wrong?" Brenna asked, worry lacing her features.

"Just a well-baby appointment I have to reschedule. No big deal." He started typing a reply to ask for an appointment the following week, when camp would be over. He could not leave Brenna alone during pickup or drop-off. She needed him.

The moment Owen's phone pinged with an incoming text message, Brenna straightened and questioned why she was at lunch with him. And his baby, for crying out loud. Making it seem like they were a little family or something. She gazed around the diner, hoping no one actually thought they were on a date. What had Emma, his sister-in-law, thought when she'd discovered them cozied up at this table?

His scrunched forehead was so cute. She shook off the attraction. Was she falling for him all over again? She reached for Lulu but remembered she had left the dog at home since most restaurants didn't prefer animals in their eateries. Instead, she pushed away from the table and the irresistible man. She couldn't fall for a man still mourning his late wife.

"Drat this autocorrect," Owen stated as he pecked away on his phone, making an adorably frustrated face.

"Why do you have to reschedule?"

"It's on Wednesday during afternoon pickup."

Her mouth fell open at the thought of him not being there for pickup. But then she turned the idea over in her mind. What if she used this as a test? Her final test to see if she could move on with her life and start to make some type of employment decision.

"Why don't you keep it," she said. His head snapped up, and he gazed at her with such concern that her heart almost burst from the attention. "Someday I have to handle life on my own. I'm feeling stronger. Why not now?"

She could handle herself. Anyway, there were loads of volunteers around, just in case.

He wavered. She could tell he was about to dispute her. "I insist," she said. "The whole point of camp was to figure out if I could get on with my life and get back into the workforce. This will be a good test." She put as much excitement into her voice as she could. Because she wanted this chance. But at the same time, she wanted Owen there for emotional support.

"If you're sure." The care covering his face warmed her.

"I am. It's settled." She gave him a nod, trying to make him believe she was okay with being alone for Wednesday afternoon pickup.

"Okay." Owen slid his phone back into his pocket. Their waitress came and took away their empty plates. "Hey, congratulations on the new bakery order from Mabel."

Heat rose in her cheeks as she thought of the diner owner's request. She'd been shocked to hear Mabel request even more baked goods. "Good thing camp is almost over, because I'm not sure I could keep up with my baking orders and still do camp."

He covered her hand with his. "That is so exciting." His eyes danced in merriment. She basked in his delight. How should she take his affection? Did he mean anything by it or was he just thrilled for a friend?

She pushed her worries away and focused on all the baking requests. They started clicking in her mind and her excitement built. Maybe she'd been afraid, but she hadn't allowed herself to consider the what-if of accepting all these jobs. Could she fulfill all these orders and still work some type of full-time job? Perhaps she was overcommitting herself.

"With the Morning Grind and Emma and Mabel's expanded orders, maybe you could actually turn your hobby into a business," Owen stated.

She sucked in a surprised breath at his comment, then quickly wondered if it was at all possible. Man, it would be cool to bake for a living. But after the attack, could she be her own boss?

"No, Owen, I'm not brave enough to take on something this big."

"Don't let the past define you. You are stronger than you think. Much stronger." His words wrapped around her chest, and she contemplated the past few weeks. Since camp had started, her accomplishments surpassed what she'd thought possible only months earlier. Maybe he was right. Maybe she was more resilient than she gave herself credit for.

Evie started to fidget, so Owen turned his attention to his daughter. There was something amazingly glorious about a man holding a baby. And the tender expression on his face proved Evie had him wrapped around her tiny pinkie. Brenna had always been drawn to him, but with a baby, he was downright irresistible. He was the whole package.

Brenna grimaced. Ugh, she was falling for him, wasn't she? She shook the errant notion from her head. If she'd learned nothing else from that stupid home invasion, it was that she had the power to steer her thoughts in a different direction. All she had to do was ignore her growing attraction to Owen, and it would go away. So instead, she focused on her growing list of baking orders.

"If I start a baking business," she asked, "do you think your brother would be willing to do my books for me?" Carter McCaw was not only an accountant but also Owen's brother.

"I can talk to him," he said. If Carter agreed, how much would he charge? The pressure on her shoulders lifted at the thought of someone else handling the finances for her. Could she really turn selling baked goods into a career?

Owen continued to tend to Evie. He was such an attentive father. And to think he didn't realize how much Cora and Wade adored him. He should be leaning into their support, not worried they were disappointed in him.

"Things seem to be going well with your parents," she stated.

"You think so?" The topic brought worry lines to his forehead. When she nodded, the crinkles disappeared a little. "I probably shouldn't be so sensitive about them, but preparing for the Bible lessons has taught me so much. I was mad at my parents for not supporting my decision to go into the military. That was such a childish reaction."

His comment made her think about her relationship with her own parents. "How so?"

"They were trying to protect me from what they thought could bring me danger. It's that unconditional love thing." He shot her a crooked smile, slid his credit card under the bill tray clip and pushed it to the edge of the table.

She wished her parents had tried to protect her. Instead, they pulled her into every fight and forced her to pick sides.

"You know, your parents love you, Brenna. They just don't show it the same way my parents do."

She tried to smile but knew it didn't reach her eyes. "I don't think so. My mother never wanted kids. And then my dad was injured." She shook her head. "It's a mess."

"I saw your mother at the grocery store the other day."

"You did?" Brenna wanted to know if her mother had asked about her but kept her mouth closed. The truth would hurt too much.

"She asked after you. Apparently, she heard about the break-in and attack and seemed worried about you." She and her mother had an understanding. Her mother didn't butt into Brenna's life and in return, Brenna didn't bug her mother about letting her father walk all over her.

"What did you tell her?"

"The truth. You are doing great. It was a horrible situation, but you are strong and have weathered the storm. She was happy to hear that." Her heart gave a little leap to hear her mother sounded like she cared. "When she walked away, she was wiping tears from her cheeks."

Wow. That was a lot of information she hadn't expected to hear. Brenna let all that settle in. She'd been afraid to visit her parents when she'd returned to Serenity. Cora had reached out to her over Christmas break about camp and Brenna had told her everything. The older woman had offered their garage apartment and Brenna had packed and driven back the next day. She'd been so broken she'd been unable to deal with spending even a minute with her parents. But now? Maybe she should visit them. Maybe she should set things right, as right as they could be.

Her chest tightened at the very thought of going to her childhood home. She wanted to reach for Lulu, but her emotional support dog was not here. Time to change the subject. So she filled Owen in on the coffee meeting she had with Isabella this past week.

"Before we parted ways she asked if we could do a Bible study," Brenna said, still in shock that the teen trusted her enough to ask. She didn't feel capable in the least, but she'd jumped at the chance. She and Isabella had already set up their next meeting.

"That's so exciting. If you want a Bible study book recommendation, let me know." She did, so they discussed a few options. Owen sent her a link to her three favorite suggestions. She'd have to go to the bookstore to peek at them before she made her selection.

Evie started squirming like she wanted out of the high chair.

"We should get going," she said, though she could spend hours more talking with Owen.

Since he had already paid their bill, they gathered their things. Well, Brenna slid her purse onto her shoulder and he collected the extraneous baby toys and bottle and shoved them in his backpack before securing smiling Evie in her car seat.

Could she actually make a living from selling her baked goods? Her pulse quickened at the idea. At least she'd discovered something she enjoyed doing, but now she'd have to figure out if she could support herself if she started her own business.

Owen slung the backpack over his shoulder and lifted the carrier. "Are you sure about Wednesday?" The worry in his eyes turned her to mush. Even though a sliver of doubt about being left alone for Wednesday pickup took hold and shook her like a rag doll, she touched his hand and squeezed, keeping her facial expression neutral so he wouldn't guess how petrified she was of him not being there.

"I'll be fine. Pickup is like ten minutes long. What can happen in that amount of time?" She chuckled, but on the inside, her stomach churned. Weeks ago, when she'd told Owen about her past, she'd begun relying on him. And he'd been her trusty helper all along.

She hoped she wasn't jumping the gun. Sure, it was likely they wouldn't have any incidents. But would dealing with pickup bring about a panic attack? She twisted her hands.

She hadn't had a full-blown panic attack since camp had started. And the last thing she wanted was to backslide.

Chapter Twelve

❧

The next afternoon, Brenna rushed down her apartment steps, eager to go horseback riding with Owen. Lulu trotted beside her, tongue lolling. She was probably excited not to have her vest on.

Brenna spotted Owen in the barn, tossing a saddle over a pretty Appaloosa standing quietly in the cross-ties. The solid muscles under his shirt rippled beneath the faded fabric. She attempted to avert her gaze, but he was too appealing.

His expression lit up when he saw her. The crinkle around his eyes hadn't been there in high school, but she liked how he had aged. Somehow, he'd become more handsome as the years had passed. And somehow she'd begun to fall for him again. That was assuming she'd ever truly gotten over him.

"Lulu gets to come along without her vest, huh?" He reached down and tousled the dog's fur. "And you with your cowboy boots and hat on?" She didn't have much of her high school wardrobe, but the boots and Stetson had stayed with her through every move. The memories were worth keeping them. She had no idea she'd use them again one day.

She posed and then twirled. "I'm a cowgirl for a day."

"Nice. We missed you at brunch." She loved the wide smile her antics had provoked.

Her hand flew to her lips. "So sorry. I meant to tell someone, but the morning just got away from me." Should she tell him she'd actually visited her parents? He was trustworthy, and it would be nice to hash out what had happened, so she dove in.

While he tightened the girth and adjusted the stirrups, she explained how the sermon had prompted her to drive by her parents' house. She had thought she was just driving by, but her mother had been on the porch looking so forlorn that Brenna had stopped before she could think. His brows rose in surprise, but the rest of his features gave her the resolve to finish the story.

"My mother stood up as soon as I pulled over and shock covered her face. I could tell she had spotted me," Brenna said. "At that point, I had to get out of the car. No more hiding." She reached for Lulu, thankful her dog had her vest on this morning so she didn't have to explain to her mother. Owen moved closer and took her trembling hand.

"That must have been so hard. How long has it been since you've seen her?"

"I've come and visited for a few hours from time to time over the years. But I haven't been to see my parents since the break-in. I just didn't feel strong enough to handle them."

"Are you okay?" At his concern, she nodded, now bursting to get the visit details off her chest.

"My father was at Fellowship Church. Apparently, the town has a service that picks him and his wheelchair up, so that's nice," she said. "My mother thinks it's healthy for them to have some alone time from each other so they don't fight as much. Sunday mornings are their time apart every week."

"Nice."

"Then she briefly apologized for all the fighting that had happened in my childhood." Owen squeezed her hand and gave her an encouraging smile. Brenna would remember her mother's apology forever, because part of her had been blaming herself for the fighting and discord in their house.

"She told me that she'd been thinking and praying for me ever since I returned to town over the Christmas holidays." Tears threatened, but Brenna pushed them back. This was a happy moment, and she didn't want to ruin it. "Then she asked how I was doing and I honestly told her." Owen engulfed her in a hug, and she breathed in the faint aroma of aftershave that clung to him. This was where she wanted to be. He leaned back and when their gazes collided, a hum of attraction snagged her.

"Congratulations on the courage to visit your childhood home and talk to your mother."

"I'm so glad I did. The visit was cathartic for me." She squeezed his hand, grateful they were friends again so she could share this exciting news with him. "Though I'll never have a relationship with my parents like you do with yours, somehow the visit today healed a small part of my worry that I'd been part of the dysfunctional problem."

"Oh, Brenna, the dysfunction in your household had nothing to do with you. You were just caught in the crosshairs."

"You think?"

"I do. Are you okay?" The concern in his eyes warmed her core. She liked being with a man who cared for her well-being. It felt good. She nodded.

"I'm so proud of you," he told her. The look on his face spoke volumes. She could tell he was proud of her. She was certainly proud of herself. Better yet, she loved that he listened to her. Truly listened, not simply thinking about what to say next. She'd missed that about him.

"Thanks." Ah, the heaviness she'd felt toward her parents had vanished.

"Ready for the trail ride?"

"Oh, yes. Today feels like a celebration." She grinned, a giddiness overtaking her.

He smiled and handed her the reins of the pretty horse he'd just tacked, their fingers tangling for a moment.

"This one's yours. Let's meet right outside the barn." He gave her a smile that flipped her stomach over, then unhitched his horse from the further cross-ties and followed her out of the barn. Their boots and horse hooves tapped across the concrete walkway. As she exited the building, sunlight heated her face.

"How about I give you a leg up?" He clasped his hands together and stooped down, the sun creating an almost halo effect around his face. She put her booted foot in his hands and swung her other leg over the calm Appaloosa. He patted her jean-clad leg and then mounted his steed while Lulu danced around the horses.

Brenna licked her lips and questioned her sanity. Why had she thought spending an afternoon alone with Owen was a smart move? She was starting to become attracted to the man and time together wouldn't make her growing feelings evaporate. She darted a glance at him as he adjusted his stirrups.

Man, Owen looked good in a saddle. She gave a second look at his horse, who was much taller than hers and chestnut in color.

"Is that Cinnamon?"

"Yes." He chuckled. "Good eye. I was pleasantly surprised to see he was still around and very healthy."

She squeezed her heels into the horse's sides as he rode alongside her, and they started their journey through the pastures. They chatted about their mornings as they walked through the cow pastures, Owen expertly opening each gate they came across.

Lulu loped alongside the horses, chasing butterflies and even a bird that was determined to fly low. Brenna was thrilled her dog was having fun because she worked so hard.

When Owen closed the final gate, they trotted along the dirt path between the fence line and the trees. It felt good to have the breeze blowing against her face and her hair streaming behind her. Freeing. Lulu ran in front of them as though she knew the destination.

They reached the stream and dismounted. Owen loosely tied both sets of reins to a hitching post.

He brushed leaves and twigs off a wooden

bench that had recently been installed and waved her over. After she sat, he settled beside her. Their legs touched, and she felt the heat from his thigh. A month ago, she would have scooted away, afraid to fall for a man she might never feel at ease with. But now, the thought of trusting a man didn't scare her as much. Or at least, trusting this man.

She tried to enjoy the moment, but lately, being near Owen got her flustered. Lulu pushed her nose at Brenna. She patted the dog and pointed to the enticing stream. Lulu gave her one last glance before trotting off to investigate the water.

"When do you start your police officer's job?" She'd finally gotten used to his chosen career. As a teen, she'd run away from him in fear. Now she stood firm. She wanted to find out where this relationship was headed because Owen was the man of her dreams. This time she wouldn't let him slip through her fingers.

He moved next to her and gave her a quizzical look. "What do you mean? I told you I'm looking for work outside of law enforcement."

"What about the offer from Chief Barker?"

"Though that unexpected offer was amazing, I rejected it." She sucked in a breath at his words, stunned. She had assumed he'd jump at the chance.

"Oh. I thought…" She reached down and pulled some pebbles out of the running water and proceeded to throw them downstream, trying to process this lovely turn of events.

He touched her elbow. "You thought what?"

"The offer sounded too good to be true." She shrugged. "I assumed you took it."

"My decision to work in a less dangerous profession didn't change at the sound of the offer. In fact, when the police chief was here, I had great peace about my decision to walk away from law enforcement."

She shook off her fingers, wet with stream water, then wiped them dry on her jeans. Her spirits lifted because he would be working in a safer profession. Though she was still in a state of shock at the surprising news. But she didn't want to make too much of his wonderful decision, so she kept her mouth closed and listened to the gurgling water.

"You trust me, right?"

When she nodded, he leaned over and gently bumped shoulders with her. Her pulse skittered at the gentle touch.

Lulu skipped over. After Brenna gave her a pat, her companion returned to investigating the stream by sticking her snout in the water and snorting.

Owen rotated on the bench to face her. "I

talked with Carter at brunch and he said he'd be happy to take you on as a client. All he needs is receipts and bills, and he handles everything." A smile played on her lips at the thought of getting back to living her life without constant fear.

After she'd crunched the possible income and expenses, she'd determined that she could make a living from selling her baked goods. It would be tight, but doable. And with Carter handling all the math stuff, the heavy weight that had been on her shoulders lifted. Delight swelled in her chest. She was really going to become an entrepreneur and start her very own baking business!

She couldn't help herself. She reached out to hug him. She enjoyed being in his strong and capable arms. And his scent was simply intoxicating. But as soon as his hair tickled her cheek, she jumped back. What was she doing? She almost shook her head. She had no idea if he liked her as more than a friend. Heat warmed her cheeks. Why had she thrown herself at him like that?

But before she knew it, he roped her back in and pressed his lips against hers.

A calm rippled through her. He tightened his hold on her, closing the gap between them, and deepened the kiss.

Kissing Owen felt right. He was so strong and capable. She snuggled into him, like on a cold winter's night. She had never thought she'd be with a man. Trust a man. But here she was. And she was enjoying it much more than she'd ever imagined.

Perhaps he did like her as more than a friend. She wasn't sure, but she did know one thing— she was falling hard for him. Again.

Maybe she should stop fighting it and simply savor the moment.

Owen leaned back and gazed into Brenna's eyes. They twinkled with interest, so he kissed her again. Her lips were pure bliss.

After Willow, he hadn't thought he'd fall in love again, but God had surprised him by bringing him and Brenna back to Serenity and into each other's arms.

He had missed Brenna. Their conversations. The future they never got to have. He furrowed his brow that he'd have intense thoughts about anyone other than Willow. Guilt about his attraction to Brenna so soon after he'd lost his wife, rose again, gnawing at him.

Lulu barked, and the sound broke their embrace. Brenna looked up at him with surprise covering her face. "What was that?"

"When a girl and a boy like each other very much…"

She smacked his arm, and he held his triceps,

pretending it hurt. So she hit him again. Then she laughed and lifted her chin to the sky. The dappled sun glinted off her long blond hair waving in the light breeze. He grinned. Boy, he had missed this playfulness. This lighthearted mood.

The fast-moving stream gurgled away as sunlight peeked through leaves in the trees, creating a feeling of seclusion. As though what happened here might stay here. When she looked back at him, he got caught in those mesmerizing blue eyes and smiled at her.

"Okay." He knew she deserved an answer to her serious question. "The kiss was my way of saying I like you and I'd like to see where this will lead."

"And I might like that," she whispered with a shy smile.

But was kissing Brenna the smartest choice? His wife had only been gone six months, and that didn't seem long enough to move on. He slid away just a little, creating a bit of distance between them as shame wound around his core. Though grief had taken its toll, his growing interest in Brenna made him wonder if he was finally coming out the other side.

He hoped so. He had loved Willow with every fiber of his being, but she wouldn't want him to linger in grief for too long.

Even though it didn't feel natural, he allowed

himself to envision a future with Brenna. Maybe build a house on the plot of land his parents had put aside for him. Marry her. If God blessed them, perhaps have a few more children. Assuming Brenna cared for him like that.

He enjoyed the silent moment, listening to the stream and Lulu splashing her way toward them. Could he put his past hurts and fears away and move forward?

"Before camp started, I was leery of working with you," she stated.

"And now?"

"I think we make a good team." She played with her fidget ring and he hoped the movement was simply a habit rather than nervousness about their potential relationship.

"Same." He bumped her lightly with his shoulder and a grin grew on her face. She was a different person than the unsure woman he'd reconnected with nearly six weeks ago. "You faced your fears. I'm proud of you, Sunshine." He startled at the term of endearment that slipped out—he'd used it when they'd dated. Pink climbed up around her neck. Apparently, she hadn't minded the moniker. Once again, he was struck by how her personality had emerged since camp started. How she'd begun dressing more confidently. And how she'd started the business of her dreams with her passion for baking.

Brenna pulled out a racquetball and instantly Lulu was at her feet, hopping up and down. She threw the ball. Lulu raced after it, splashing in the water as she chased it down.

He pulled out his phone. No new message from Pastor Reed, the head pastor from the Love Valley church looking to start a youth program. He likely took Sunday afternoons off. He had probably preached this morning and was on the couch watching baseball or napping right now. Except Owen had left his first message for the man a week ago.

"Expecting a call?" Brenna asked.

Excitement lifted in Owen's chest over the new youth program the pastor was thinking about. He told her about the open position for a youth pastor who would create a new mentoring program for tween and teen boys.

"I've left the head pastor a couple of messages and haven't heard back. I'm eager to talk with him about volunteering." The enthusiasm he had back when he and Willow had been planning their program for at-risk youth hadn't diminished. If anything, it had increased exponentially. And he wanted to help in any way he could.

"I'm excited for you," she said.

"Not that I'll have time to volunteer as a single parent, but since we helped start an outreach program at our last church and learned a lot, I thought I could share our experiences." He pocketed his phone and shrugged. Building that volunteer team with their pastor had been an intense, yet gratifying, time.

"So smart. That way, they won't fall for the same pitfalls you did." Her magnetic eyes drew him in.

This conversation made Owen realize they weren't the same people they'd been ten years ago. They'd each gone through life and experiences. They'd grown and learned. Yet they still had a comfortable rapport between them.

"Where's Evie today?" Lulu returned with a dripping ball, grinning as she dropped the toy in Brenna's lap. The dog danced, eyes on the ball, while she waited for Brenna's next move.

"With my parents." This single-parent thing wasn't as hard as he'd feared it would be. Yet he knew that living with his parents and not having a real job was masking how difficult it would be to raise Evie alone.

Brenna tossed the ball, but there was something in her expression. Worry? Unease? He wasn't sure. Maybe she was having second thoughts about their kiss.

"You seem concerned," Owen said. He swallowed, wondering if he'd been smart to kiss her. Pink splotches appeared on her cheeks. Man, she was adorable. The ghosting back in high school came to mind, but he pushed it away. It was in the past. Hadn't he already decided they were different people now?

"Edith caught me before church and told me she'd help with funding the purchase of the bakery, but I don't know…" She hopped off the bench and moved to the edge of the stream.

He followed her. "I thought you were happy selling your baked goods? Seems like your business is taking off."

"Well, part of the deal is that I could live in that cozy apartment above the bakery that always smells like sweet treats."

He blinked and then slowly shook his head. "Brenna, are you feeling pressured to move out of my parents' garage apartment?"

"No," she said quickly. "Well, kind of." The uncertainty on her face twisted his gut. He could live anywhere; Brenna on the other hand, needed the stability of staying in the garage apartment. At least for now.

"Well, worry no more. I'm moving into Laney's house. You know, the one she inherited from her aunt and uncle that's now vacant?"

"Wait. Are you doing this for me?" She cocked her head to the side as though skeptical he had honorable reasons to move out of his parents' house.

"Partly." He grinned. "But mostly because it's time for me and Evie to start our lives without a safety net." He sobered at the thought of doing without his mother's constant support.

"When did this happen?"

"I asked Laney about it a week ago and we hashed out the details." He moved a loose tendril of silky hair away from her cheek, resisting the temptation to kiss her again. "I checked it out yesterday afternoon. It'll be perfect for me and Evie." At least, he hoped. He was trusting Evie was too young to have taken too much of a liking to his parents' home. Hopefully, he could parent her all by himself without messing up.

"But I thought the house was used by the caterers and the bridal parties."

He waved her comment off. "No. Only the first floor. She renovated the second floor into a spacious two-bedroom apartment with a kitchenette. You know, back when she thought she would live there. Before she married Ethan. Anyway, I'm moving in as soon as summer camp is over." Brenna pressed a palm to her heart, clearly relieved she could remain in his parents' garage apartment.

"But what about the loud music and boisterous people talking during the receptions?" Her brow crinkled in concern. Oh, how he loved that she worried about the well-being of his daughter. "The noise from those weddings will keep Evie up." She tossed the dripping ball into the creek for Lulu to chase down.

"Now that Laney has three children and another on the way, she only hosts one wedding a week during the season. Off-season maybe one a month. On the wedding days, we'll just have a sleepover at Memaw and Pops'." He tried to infuse excitement into his voice, but in reality he was worried he'd be a failure at parenting alone. "It's been decided." And since he didn't want Brenna to feel pressured about leaving his parents' garage apartment, he'd have to follow through and move out even though it sounded scary.

She grinned. "Thank you. You are too sweet." He got lost in her sparkling gaze and before he knew it, he had his arms around her again and she sank into his embrace.

He had never stopped loving Brenna and now hoped they could have a future together. Except, were things happening too quickly?

He had expected the dominoes of doubt to topple over, but a few uncertainties remained. He wasn't convinced moving on was right. Maybe it never would be.

Chapter Thirteen

After the well-baby checkup on Wednesday, Owen settled Evie in her car seat. "Ninetieth percentile on weight, baby girl. Good job." He pressed a soft kiss to her forehead. She responded with "da" and he waited, but she just repeated it as a single syllable. Oh, for the day she said *Dada* for the first time. He recalled the conversation he'd had with Brenna not too long ago about Evie's speaking progress and her interest in his baby's developments. Part of him longed to share parenting with someone, the good, the bad and the ugly.

The kisses they'd shared over the weekend proved his feelings for Brenna were stronger than ever. His thoughts drifted to summer camp, and he checked his watch. Afternoon pickup was about to happen. He hoped Brenna would realize her own strength. He settled in the driver's seat, frustrated that the drive to the Triple C Ranch from Love Valley would take too long for him to arrive before pickup was complete.

His cell phone vibrated. Before starting the truck, he pulled the device out and spotted a text from Mark Reed, the pastor from Love Valley. Before excitement could take hold, he pushed the emotion away. Though passionate about the volunteer work, as a single father, unfortunately he didn't have the required time to commit. He set aside his personal disappointment and focused on the message.

Pastor Reed apologized for not returning his call, but he'd been on vacation. He wanted to know if Owen could meet him sometime this week. Owen replied he was in Love Valley. Would right now work?

The church was literally on his way home. And since there was no way he'd be back to help Brenna with pickup, he might as well knock this meeting out. He hoped the pastor agreed to the meeting. Then he could share what he'd learned from his prior church experience. Maybe that would help the pastor. And perhaps helping in this little way would take the desire to volunteer for the program away from Owen's heart.

Pastor Reed replied with the thumbs-up emoji, so Owen plugged Redeemer Church into his maps app and put his truck in gear. When he arrived at the church, he pulled Evie's car seat out. The doctor appointment must have tired her out because she was sound asleep.

An older gentleman with white sideburns and copper hair held open the glass door of the office building. The crinkles in the corners of his eyes and mouth professed to a lifetime of laughter.

Owen shook the man's hand as the pastor introduced himself. They exchanged pleasantries as they wound their way to the back, where Pastor Reed's office was located. Wow, this was bigger than his home church in Serenity.

"How old is your baby?"

"Six months." Then Owen briefly explained that Willow had passed away at the same time their baby was born. Pastor Reed gave his condolences and then commented on how adorable Evie was, which broke the ice. Talking about Willow's car accident was never easy.

"So I hear you are interested in serving with the youth?"

"As a single father, I won't have much time to devote to volunteering, but I wanted to share my experience from when I helped launch a similar program at my home church in North Carolina." They briefly discussed that Owen had been in the military and, most recently a police officer, but was currently seeking safer employment.

"I'd love to hear anything that will help for when we start our program." Pastor Reed had such a warm and welcoming face that it was easy to open up and share.

Owen didn't hold back. Even though he'd not be able to serve here because he didn't have sufficient time, he explained about the role he and Willow had at their church in North Carolina. Some of the pitfalls they'd experienced during start-up and execution. Then he described the youth program at the rec center he and Willow had been working with and how the program they'd wanted to start had targeted inner-city kids and was laser focused on ten-to thirteen-year-olds, but would still accommodate older teens. As Owen talked, he became more animated and excited. His heart thumped in his chest as he spoke about his passion.

"I love that," Pastor Reed said, those laugh lines around his eyes crinkling at his broad smile.

He questioned Owen about how he served at his church in North Carolina. Then he drilled into the youth program and how Owen had participated in the beginnings of that project. Owen hadn't realized that his experiences would be so interesting to the pastor, but he didn't mind all the questions. Beside Evie, his love of serving with teens was his second favorite topic.

Pastor Reed leaned back in his chair and gave Owen a nod. "Well, Owen, I think you are the man we've been looking for to fill our youth pastor's role."

He put his hands up, palms out. "I'm not a pastor, I'm a police officer," he exclaimed.

The pastor chuckled. "That explains it. A police officer's role is very similar to a pastor's. Though pastors have a safer job, both roles require significant interpersonal communication skills."

He felt a little dizzy at Pastor Reed's statement. As he let the surprising words roll around for a few minutes, he found he didn't hate the idea, but he wasn't qualified in the least.

"I can tell this has surprised you, but let me tell you more about the job." Pastor Reed proceeded to list the job responsibilities to Owen, along with the perk of flexible hours. Then he named the salary.

Owen had already determined that with Evie, he would be best suited to a job that gave him some flexibility. As a single parent, he didn't want to work overtime or have a long commute. So the option to work some from home and have flexible hours were perfect. The salary was comparable to his police officer's pay and he might even be able to bring Evie to church events as long as she cooperated.

But a pastor? He shook his head. Before he could reject the outrageous offer, Pastor Reed leaned forward, placed his elbows on his desk and jumped in.

"I know this has come as a bit of a surprise, but think it over and converse with the Lord about it. I promise that even if you don't accept the job, you are welcome to help the youth pastor that we'll eventually hire."

They rose and shook hands. On the way back to his car, Owen was in a fog. Pastor? Boy, his brothers would rib him if he accepted the job.

But pastor? He just couldn't get over the idea of accepting a role he wasn't qualified for. Or was he?

He secured Evie in the car and then settled in the driver's seat once again. He couldn't wait to tell Brenna all about this opportunity. Would she laugh or tell him that it sounded like the perfect fit?

Lately, her eyes gleamed like they had in high school, and the look of fear that used to cover her face had vanished. Seemed like helping run camp had gotten her over the hump and she was ready to jump back into life.

Would she be interested in doing life with him? Hope curled quietly in his chest.

Because the more he dwelled on that memorable kiss and how much he enjoyed spending time with Brenna, the more he realized he was in love with her. Head over heels in love.

And he wanted to spend the rest of his days with her.

Before he started driving, he turned on the Serenity police scanner. For some reason, the occasional chatter of law enforcement calmed Owen. He'd always be a police officer at heart, though God had a different plan for the next season of his life. Now it was time for Owen to rely on God to tell him what that might be.

A squawk sounded on his phone and the dispatcher ordered a fire truck and EMS squad to a burning smell on Madison. Owen figured it was likely burnt toast, but sending authorities to check it out was never a bad idea.

He pulled out of the parking lot and pointed his truck in the direction of the Triple C Ranch, holding the steering wheel much too tight as the shocking conversation with Pastor Reed rolled around in his head. He wasn't pastor material, was he?

His stomach churned with the life-altering decision in front of him.

Back at camp, one child hadn't been picked up, making Brenna's stomach wobble. She patted the girl's back as Lulu stuck close by. Brenna could tell her dog was reading her nervousness, but everything would be fine once little Lucy's mother arrived. She practiced her breathing techniques and tried to focus on something good. Owen announcing he rejected the police officer's job popped into her head and made her smile for a moment. She had been shocked. And relieved. Though she'd come to terms with being involved with someone who faced danger daily, she was thrilled that wouldn't be the case.

"I'm heading over to the barn to check on the status of cleanup," Hazel, her lead afternoon volunteer, stated. The volunteers must all be in the barn preparing for tomorrow morning. "Are you okay here?" The concern in her voice warmed Brenna's core. She'd come to know and care about the volunteers, as well as the campers, this summer. She'd miss their daily interactions when camp ended on Friday.

"Thanks, Hazel, I've got things here. Go ahead." The afternoon camp had gone according to schedule with Owen missing—other than Lucy, who had yet to be picked up. But her mother was probably running late. She had an infant and a broken marriage, so she was always a little harried.

In preparation for the morning campers, Brenna finished pushing the picnic tables back into position. Was it just a few days ago that Owen had kissed her? She touched her lips at the memory.

Were they rekindling their relationship? She wasn't sure what to make of what happened Sunday afternoon. If she were honest, she was drawn to Owen. Except allowing their relationship to unfold was part scary, part exciting.

"How come my mommy isn't here?" Lucy asked, her lower lip trembling. Brenna laid a supportive hand on the camper's shoulder and tried to push away the memory of the kiss. Maybe she should get the girl's mother's phone number and give her a call to make sure things were okay.

"It's okay, Lucy, your mom probably got tied up. She'll be here any minute." Brenna squatted down and eyed the teary-eyed girl. "How about you help me clean up the kitchen? I think there might be a couple of cookies left over." Lucy's face brightened at the mention of a treat.

As she reached her hand out to the girl, a beater pickup truck roared into the lot, spraying gravel everywhere when it screeched to a stop in front of her. A big, brawny man sat behind the wheel and looked down at her with bloodshot eyes. She straightened and pulled Lucy behind her. Lulu appeared at her side, ready to help. Who was this man and where was Lucy's sweet mama?

He hand-cranked his window down, and country music blasted from the interior. "Come on, Lucy, get in the car," the man slurred over the noise. Brenna felt the little girl shudder behind her. This must be Lucy's estranged father.

Brenna had all but memorized the camper's consent forms and knew Lucy had a mother, grandmother and a neighbor authorized to pick her up. They had strict rules about releasing children to only authorized people. Since Brenna hadn't heard differently from Lucy's mother, Lucy would remain at camp until Brenna saw one of them.

He reached onto his dash and must have turned off the radio, because the music stopped and an eerie silence settled over them. Her gut clenched, cold and uneasy. Why had she told Hazel to leave?

She cast a furtive glance around. The area was empty except for her, Lucy and this man. Unlike the home invasion, there wasn't a lamp, or any weapon, at her disposal right now. What she wanted to do was run. But she knew Lucy's little legs wouldn't be able to keep up, and the girl was much too large for Brenna to carry. Anyway, turning and fleeing would only upset this man more, and he'd likely charge after them. She gulped away her fear and made her stance wider as she felt Lucy cowering behind her.

"Come on, kid, let's get going."

"Hello," Brenna said, thankful her voice wasn't shaky like her insides. She tried for her teacher voice and composure, hoping to catch the man off guard. All the while going through all the helpful tips she'd learned from the numerous self-defense classes she'd taken recently. "You must be Lucy's father. I'm sorry, but I don't remember who is on her approved pickup list. Just let me run to the office and grab her card. I'll be back in a jiff." Before he could say anything, she turned and pushed Lucy in front of her while dialing 911 on her cell phone. Lulu stuck by their side as they rushed toward the office.

When the dispatcher answered, Brenna recognized the voice as a fellow church parishioner who served in childcare on Sundays and loved on Evie when she could. "Marie, this is Brenna Park at Victory Youth Camp." She spoke softly, not wanting to reveal to Lucy's father that she was nervous. "Could you send someone off duty to the Triple C please? I have an unapproved parent here and a bad feeling about this situation." Just having Marie on the line comforted her.

"Sure thing, Brenna. Just stay on the phone with me." Brenna punched the speakerphone button and reached for the office door as she heard heavy boots behind her. Her adrenaline spiked at the nearness of the noise. She stuck the phone in her back pocket as Lucy started shrieking. The footsteps sounded close, so she ripped open the door and shoved Lucy in, instructing her to lock the door and not let anyone in.

Her heart pounded as she scrambled to the large open gathering space as quickly as she could. She wasn't sure what this man's intentions were, but she wanted him as far away from Lucy as possible. Lulu stuck beside Brenna and she reached down to pet her companion, trying to calm the dog and herself at the same time.

Except the man didn't follow her. He strode to the office door and began pounding. Yelling for Lucy to let him in.

Brenna's hands trembled as she fought her brain to come up with the right words to say to get the man over here and away from defenseless Lucy.

But her brain seemed frozen as she held back the frightened scream in her throat.

Chapter Fourteen

While driving toward Serenity, the police scanner in Owen's truck roared to life with Brenna's scared voice. He glanced at the scanner, shocked to hear the woman he loved. He listened closely and his chest tightened at the fear laced through her words. What was going on?

He raised the volume to the highest level as his stomach churned with this turn of events. He slowed the car to concentrate on driving and what was being said.

Something about the arrival of someone who was not an approved parent. Then she stated she had a bad feeling about the man. A cold knot twisted in Owen's gut. Was she blowing a normal situation out of control or was something nefarious happening at Victory Youth Camp?

Right then, Evie started crying. He must have woken her by blaring the police scanner to hear more clearly.

"Shh, sweetheart, we'll be back at the ranch soon." He tried to appease her from a distance with calming words, but his insides were anything but calm. He was shaking with worry over whatever might be happening at the camp. And the safety of the woman he loved. *Please God, keep Brenna safe. Give her calming abilities to handle whatever situation she's in.*

Through Evie's screams, he heard banging on the scanner. He held his breath, trying to place the sound of the foreign commotion. Was that noise coming from the camp or the dispatcher? Probably the camp, but he couldn't tell. His heart raced.

He sped up because he couldn't hear the words on the scanner through Evie's wails. The best he could do was get back to camp ASAP.

He should have rescheduled the well-baby appointment, or at least not accepted the last-minute meeting with the pastor. He gritted his teeth. Brenna was in this situation because of him. His gut clenched tighter as guilt tangled around the knot already there. What had he been thinking?

As safely as possible, he rushed back to the Triple C, but he was still almost ten minutes away.

He could barely hear Brenna when she spoke next. Or was that the dispatcher? He couldn't tell through Evie's loud sobbing. The words were soft enough that he couldn't hear them clearly.

He wanted to slam his palms against the steering wheel, but that wouldn't help anyone. In fact, it might frighten Evie.

His body tensed as he realized his worst fear was coming true—Brenna was in danger because of him. He'd made an ill-advised decision to keep Evie's well-baby appointment, which he could have easily rescheduled for next week.

When Brenna wouldn't be relying on him.

When this strange man would not be confronting her and possibly hurting her.

As he whizzed past cow pasture after cow pasture, his grip tightened on the steering wheel. But he forced himself to stay within the speed limit.

He was so angry with himself because whatever was happening at camp was all his fault.

"Now I remember who is on Lucy's approved pickup list," Brenna called to the man, trying to keep the quaking fear from her voice. His head swung toward the gathering space and he eyed her. He looked a little wobbly. Was he drunk or something? She wasn't sure, but regardless, she wanted him away from Lucy. *Please walk away from that door and your sweet child who is probably cowering in the back corner right now. Come over here, whoever you are, and direct your anger at me. Come on*, she willed the man. She could almost see the wheels turning in his head, rotating through his limited options.

She pulled out her phone, noticing the phone app was still connected to 911. "I'll just check your name against what I have on file." She pretended to scan something on her phone while she muttered to Marie, the dispatcher, to mute herself. Brenna heard a quiet *Done*. Hopefully, this guy wouldn't guess the authorities were listening in on their conversation.

She looked up. The guy hadn't moved. But he'd stopped pounding on the door and turned to her. His interest appeared piqued.

"What did you say your last name was?" She pretended like she was scrolling on a list to get him to come to her instead of trying to break down the door where Lucy was hiding.

"I didn't say," he muttered as he started toward her. Glee that he'd abandoned trying to reach Lucy quickly turned to alarm as his long strides ate up the distance between them in no time. Her insides quivered at his approach. Or maybe they had been shaking all along, she wasn't sure.

He stepped into Brenna's personal space, forcing her to resist the urge to step back and create distance between them. If she didn't know better, she'd say his stance was aggressive. Lulu leaned against Brenna. But instead of soothing her, she was irked that she needed an emotional support dog. She didn't want the man to think she was weak—because she wasn't. Determination took over, and she lifted her chin. She was strong and could handle this situation.

She shot the man a small smile. "I take it your last name is Freeman, like Lucy's?" She made sure to enunciate clearly. That ought to give Marie some context to give to the police, assuming the dispatcher had even sent anyone out. How did they assess an emergency versus an anxious resident?

"Yep," he said. That one word let enough of his breath drift into the air for Brenna to smell alcohol. Instead of scaring her, she felt satisfaction she had taken the proper steps to protect Lucy. Even if he was being truthful and he truly was her father, Brenna couldn't let him drive in an inebriated state.

Noise to her right had her and the man glancing over. Hazel marched toward them. A couple more volunteers lagged behind. In the distance, she spotted Ethan McCaw loping in their direction, tilting his hat up with his focus on the strange man. Relief spilled through her at the reinforcements.

She swung her gaze back to the man. "First name?" Making her tone all business. At her request, he seemed to lose a bit of courage.

"Um, Bo," he said. His shoulders sagged at the sight of Ethan stepping into the pavilion. She felt like cheering because this tough guy was wilting like a tomato plant in a drought. But they weren't done yet. This guy was huge. If he wanted to, he could probably take out Ethan. And then what? She kept her intensity up. For Lucy.

"Bo Freeman," she said as she ran her finger down her phone as though looking at a list. Surely the dispatcher would hear the full name and pass it on, assuming a police officer was on his way.

"Everything okay here?" Ethan asked as he stepped up to them. Bo's shoulders collapsed even more with Ethan's close presence. She wanted to shout for joy, but kept her mouth closed.

Next thing she knew, a police siren sounded and quickly shut off as it turned into the lot. Out jumped Chief Barker, hand on his waist where his duty belt hung.

The sight of the police car seemed to sober Bo, who took a step back and apologized to Brenna and Ethan and the other volunteers before Chief Barker had the chance to even step into the pavilion.

The police chief took the man's wrist and slapped handcuffs on him. "Bo, what are you doing? You know you don't have visitation privileges with Lucy anymore. Why are you here?"

Brenna let the police handle Bo and raced to the office to comfort Lucy. When Lulu licked the little girl's face, she giggled, then asked if there were still cookies in the kitchen. Relief that Lucy was moving on from this horrendous event lifted Brenna's lips in a shaky smile.

"Of course there are, sweetie." She extended her hand to the girl, who grasped it.

They went to the kitchen and while Lucy enjoyed a cookie, Brenna called the girl's mother only to discover that she was at the hospital with Lucy's grandmother. In a grief-stricken haze, the mother had asked her ex-husband to pick up Lucy. She apologized for Bo's behavior and approved a neighbor, a mother Brenna knew from morning camp, to pick up her daughter.

When Chief Barker left with Bo in the back seat, Brenna released the breath she'd been holding. She patted Lulu and realized that even though she had been in a very disturbing situation, she hadn't panicked. Oh, she'd been concerned about the welfare of the little girl. But despite Bo invading her personal space and the threatening situation, her heart hadn't raced. In fact, she'd felt completely in control. A smile started slow but certain.

"Can I have one more?" Lucy asked, giving Brenna cute little puppy-dog eyes.

"Of course you can, sweetheart." She handed one more cookie to Lucy and hoped her ride would arrive soon, because if the girl asked for a third, she'd probably hand it over.

Another car pulled into the drive. She peeked out the kitchen window and spotted Owen's truck parked haphazardly. Her pulse galloped at the sight of the man she loved. She grinned, gave Lulu a hug and thanked God for protecting her and Lucy today. And for helping her get back to her former self. Sure, she might have episodes again, but today proved she was on the mend. And that was the whole point of helping run camp.

Right before Owen arrived at the Triple C, he passed a police car with Chief Barker at the wheel and a passenger held in the back seat. Relief flowed through Owen at the sight.

He pulled next to the pavilion and slammed his truck into Park. He jumped out and then opened the back door for airflow for Evie, who was again snoozing. Apparently, the car movement had lulled her back to sleep. He spotted Brenna emerging from the camp kitchen. Tears welled up behind his eyelids at the sight of her unhurt. He rushed over and gave her a tight hug.

He inhaled a deep breath of her rose scent, grateful for her safety. And that Bo Freeman hadn't done something stupid.

"I'm so glad you're okay," he said, then pulled

back and eyed her from head to toe. "You aren't hurt, are you? Bo didn't lay a hand on you, did he?" Her quizzical expression scared him. Maybe she'd fallen and hit the back of her head or something that wasn't visible to the eye.

"How do you even know?" she asked. He engulfed her in another hug, tighter this time. Why had he doubted moving on and marrying Brenna? He loved her more than life. She was his future. He knew that now.

"I heard the whole thing on the police scanner on my way back from Love Valley," he whispered. A fist tightened around his gut that Brenna had been in that situation because of him. He'd selfishly met Pastor Reed at Redeemer Church when he should have returned to Victory Youth Camp. Though he'd thought pickup was complete, he shouldn't have dallied. Had he driven straight here from the doctor's office, he might have intercepted Bo. Then Brenna never would have been in danger.

"Owen, I'm okay, really." She squirmed out of his arms. "I didn't have a panic attack." Her face was bright and Lulu panted by her side, looking altogether unconcerned. Certainly not the reaction Owen had expected because he'd been frantic on his drive back.

Regardless, he had put the love of his life in danger. Just like he'd done with Willow. Before he could process that thought, a sedan showed up and the mother of one of the morning campers stepped out of her car and approached Brenna.

"I'm so sorry for this," she said as a little girl who'd been standing with the women volunteers scrambled over and glued herself to the mom. "Bo can be a handful, but I'm glad Lucy is all right." Brenna thanked her for coming and gave the girl a cookie for the road while Owen returned to his car to collect his daughter. Evie was awake and batting at those dangling things hanging from the carrier handle. Her smile was sweet and innocent. Wouldn't it be nice to be happily oblivious to life's dangers? But he couldn't ignore what he'd just done.

Heart heavy, he trudged back to the pavilion and gave Ethan a grateful handshake.

"Glad I was here to help," his brother said. The statement was a sucker punch to the gut. His brother had to step in because Owen hadn't been here. He hadn't been here to protect Brenna.

And that had been the reason he had resolved not to fall in love again. How could he have been so careless to give away his heart when it should have been locked up in a vault?

Brenna waved at the sedan as it pulled away, a smile lifting her lips. With Lulu by her side, she dashed over to Owen and barreled into him, giving him a tight squeeze. It felt good to have her arms around him, but he couldn't let this continue.

No, she deserved better than him.

He had chosen work over driving his wife to the baby shower and she'd had a fatal car accident. Had he been there, the outcome may have been different. He roughed a hand over the back of his sweaty neck.

Even though he had fallen in love with Brenna, he refused to allow that love to flourish. He could not handle going through loving and losing again.

The only way to be assured of not hurting again was to put as much distance between himself and Brenna.

His chest squeezed at what he had to do.

But not right now. This embrace felt too good. He'd enjoy this last hug for another moment. Or two.

She clung to Owen—not like a lifeboat in a storm, her only hope of survival—but because she loved him. The truth settled in her core and made her smile. He completed her.

She'd dismissed him in high school out of fear and then wasted the last ten years trying to forget him. Now she was madly in love with Owen, and their bright future stood within her grasp. Especially now that she was healing from the event in her past. She sucked in a deep breath of his scent—a hint of aftershave, but mostly the fresh outdoors—thrilled to be in his arms, and allowed the embrace to deepen.

Yes, while she'd been alone with Bo, fear had tripped down her spine, but she was glad the man had shown up and made a ruckus. The incident had proven she was on the road to recovery. No, she wasn't completely healed from the home invasion, but her panic attacks were nearly gone, or at least under control. She was closer to her normal self.

Owen reached up and peeled her arms off him, then took a large step back. His lips were pinched as though he'd just eaten a lemon.

Her heart dropped. What was happening? Was he upset with her for some reason?

She missed the security of his arms around her and wanted them back. Not because she *needed* him, but because she wanted him near. It felt so free to not need someone. To feel confident enough to stand on her own. But the look on Owen's face gave her pause.

Brenna thought they cared for one another. Especially after the kiss the other day. As scary as it sounded, she was in love with Owen.

"What's happening?" she asked. He gave her a shake of his head and took another step away, creating much too much distance between them.

His dull eyes hinted that her feelings weren't reciprocated. She wanted to ask but feared his answer. His sudden indifferent demeanor was crushing her. Lulu leaned against her leg and Brenna reached for her dog, hating that she took such comfort in the softness of her fur.

Why was he withdrawing from her when she'd survived a scary situation without even the hint of a panic attack?

He turned, picked up the car carrier with Evie in it and walked away without another word. Without a glance back. As though he didn't care for her at all.

She wanted to call out to him, but for some reason, her voice didn't work. He strode into Cora and Wade's home, firmly closing the green front door behind him.

Tears stung her eyes as confusion swirled around her. What was happening? Had she said something to offend him? Did he find her too needy? She wouldn't think so, not after she'd handled the Bo situation so calmly. But why?

"He'll get over it," Ethan stated before he plopped his Stetson back on his sweaty head and turned to the barns.

She stared at Cora and Wade's front door, closed tight, and felt the urge to run up to her apartment and bake. But should she?

Maybe she should go over, open that green

door and clear the air between them. She nibbled her lower lip in indecision. No. She'd give him time to process because she sure needed some. The kiss. The realization she was in love. And her breakthrough today during a dangerous situation. It was a lot to take in.

Seemed like Owen was putting up his guard, and maybe that wasn't a bad idea. Not too long ago she'd been convinced she'd never be able to trust a man again.

A knot tightened in her gut—how had she gone and fallen in love with a man who didn't love her back?

Chapter Fifteen

Saturday morning, Owen tipped his Stetson back and gazed at the view. The rolling pastures extended as far as he could see and were dotted with cattle munching on grass. Not until returning to Serenity had he realized how much he'd missed the wide-open spaces at the Triple C.

"It sure is pretty out here, isn't it, Cinnamon?" he asked the horse that he'd grown up with. Cinnamon shook his head. The reins, lying against his withers, waved freely with his motion.

Yet Owen struggled to enjoy the moment without Brenna by his side. His chest ached that they would never seize their second chance. But going their separate ways was for the best. At least he thought so.

Yesterday, his mother had vehemently disagreed. She'd told him that hearts were a lot bigger than we gave them credit for. Then, after a pump of her eyebrows, she'd told him that if he met the right woman, she had confidence there was space in there for her. Finally, his mother had patted his chest, right where his heart sat thumping, and for a brief moment he wondered if he was wrong to push Brenna away.

His mother was a wise woman, but his heart wasn't ready for another pummeling.

Ethan trotted over and pulled his horse to a stop alongside him. "Couldn't be more stunning, could it?"

He glanced at his brother. In between moving the herd from one pasture to another, he'd hoped they'd get an opportunity to talk. It was the reason he'd jumped at the chance to help when he'd heard their father wasn't feeling well.

Owen shook out his hands, hoping some of the nervous tension would release. It didn't. After speaking with Pastor Reed yesterday evening, he was so close to accepting the youth pastor's position.

"It's gorgeous here," he said. Now, how to broach the topic without sounding desperate? He decided to just jump in.

"I was offered a job. One I don't believe I am qualified for." He proceeded to tell Ethan all about the position. How much he had loved working with the youth in North Carolina. And how the youth had his heart.

Bandit, the ranch's golden retriever, loped beside them, waiting for his next command.

"Well, pray about it, but to be honest, it sounds

like a great fit." Ethan adjusted in his saddle. The answer shocked Owen. He had expected his siblings to needle him for considering a role he was wholly unqualified for. But his brother's optimism gave Owen a little more courage to accept the role. "I always thought you sent pictures of the teens at events because you didn't yet have kids. I guess I never realized how much they meant to you. But now, looking back on the text messages that we exchanged, I can see how much you poured into the youth."

The excitement on his brother's face pushed Owen over the edge. He wanted this job. Really wanted it. To work with the youth and be paid for it? That sounded like a dream. All these years serving in ministry, he'd never considered turning what he loved into a profession. And, with Pastor Reed agreeing that attending seminary online could be part of the job, the offer had become hard to resist.

"I think I might accept the position," Owen stated. Just saying it out loud felt good.

Ethan smacked him on the back. "Congratulations, bro. I'm excited for you."

They trotted to the next gate. Even though Owen was thrilled about his new career, he missed Brenna. Sure, their relationship had only been building a short while, and they had not been an official couple or anything, but apart from her, he felt a hole in his heart. For that reason, he couldn't feel excited about accepting the youth pastor's role without her by his side.

"What's going on with you and Brenna?" At the mention of the woman he loved, Owen's throat dried up. Sure, he loved her, but she was better off without him. Why couldn't his brother see that? "Ever since the whole Bo incident, it seems like there's friction between you guys." Owen rolled his eyes, trying to make light of the sudden split. He'd hoped to keep their brief relationship under wraps. Apparently, he'd failed.

"I didn't know anyone had noticed."

Ethan raised his eyebrow. "Not only is it obvious to everyone, but Laney said Brenna dropped by on her lunch hour yesterday to ask her about it. Brenna thinks you're mad at her, but apparently she's too afraid to ask you about it."

The turmoil that had been roiling in his gut for the past four days continued.

"She was in danger Wednesday because of me," Owen spat out.

"How so?"

Was his brother going to force him to explain the obvious? He shot Ethan a quick glance, but his brother looked clueless.

"You may not know this, but I was supposed to drive Willow to the baby shower. When I had to work late, we decided I'd meet her there. Except she had the car accident." He roughed a hand over his face. "If I'd declined the overtime and gone home to drive her, Willow would still be alive."

Ethan cocked his head as though he didn't understand.

"It's my fault Willow died." Owen stated the obvious.

"No, it's not," Ethan said softly. "She died in an accident. I thought you'd come to terms with this weeks ago."

"I thought I had, but hearing Brenna's voice on the police scanner shook me." Cinnamon shifted his weight, and Owen placed his hand on the worn saddle horn. "That incident with Bo was a wake-up call. I could have lost Brenna."

Ethan gave a low whistle. "Now you are blowing things out of proportion. Brenna wasn't in any real danger. The volunteers were there, I was there, Dad was close by. It might have seemed scary to her at the moment, but Bo was just being Bo."

"I can't lose her." Except, his brain and emotions were in conflict as his stomach coiled into a tight knot at not having Brenna in his life anymore.

Ethan chuckled. "Oh, I see. You are using what happened with Willow as an excuse to run from Brenna because you are scared. But the truth is, you're afraid because you've fallen in love." Shock hit Owen as though someone had thrown a punch square in his face. Was that what he was doing—running because he was afraid? He allowed the past few days to filter through his mind like a slideshow, giving him the clear answer. How was his brother able to read him so well?

"Maybe." Owen rubbed the back of his neck where tension had gathered. "Loving and losing is heart-wrenching, and I don't think I can do it again. I won't." He had thought walking away from Brenna would resolve his fears, but instead his yearning for her kept growing.

Even though he had done the responsible thing and parted ways, all he wanted was to be with her, talk with her, spend time with her. But he couldn't go through that pain again. His brother caught his attention and pierced him with a look that made him sit straighter in the saddle.

"What did God teach you," his brother asked, "right at the start of camp, when you were preparing for your first week of Bible lessons?"

Owen thought back to that time and how scared he was about teaching Bible lessons when he hadn't stayed all that close to God since high school. During those first few weeks of camp, his relationship with the Lord had reignited.

"I hadn't kept God a priority in my life."

"Bingo. Did you make the decision to end things with Brenna on your own, or did you consult with God?"

Owen frowned. He didn't like where this conversation was headed. "I guess you could say I didn't consult with God." He waited for the berating words, but they didn't come. Instead, Ethan extended gentleness.

"I get it. You are afraid. But you might want to stop running." He made a clicking noise and moved away, leaving Owen with his thoughts.

Ugh. He hated it when someone else was able to drill down and find the truth so easily. Why did his older brother have to be so wise?

Was it right to walk away for fear of *maybe* getting hurt one day?

He pressed his heels into Cinnamon to follow his brother.

Ethan was right. The only way to overcome his fears was to rely on God, but could he? He wanted to because he loved Brenna more than the air he breathed. And he knew beyond a shadow of a doubt that God didn't want His children living in fear.

A serene peace flooded Owen.

He wasn't sure what would happen in the future, but if God gave him the confidence he needed, he wanted Brenna back. For good.

* * *

Saturday morning, Brenna sprayed cleaner on the stainless steel counters and dried them with a soft cloth. The overhead lights reflected on the shiny surface, creating a sunny glow, but her mood was anything but sunny.

She gazed around the industrial kitchen. Why hadn't Edith left more of a mess? Brenna had already prepped everything for tomorrow, washed all the dishes and emptied the dishwashers. Nothing left but to leave and return to the Triple C.

She frowned, slid her purse strap on her shoulder and dimmed the lights. The final few days of camp had been exhilarating, but after Owen had pulled away from her and rejected her completely, the excitement was no longer there.

She didn't want to return to the Triple C Ranch, not with her and Owen on the outs. Sure, he planned on moving to Laney's, but she sensed he'd decided on relocating to ease Brenna's guilt about living in his parents' garage apartment. Who knew? Maybe he wouldn't move. After all, the ranch was his home. Maybe she should find somewhere else to live and give him the space he needed. Even though she wasn't going to purchase the bakery, maybe Edith would still let her rent out the second-floor apartment. It couldn't hurt to ask.

The doors swished as Edith entered the space. "Where are you going? A friend is here to visit with you."

Indecision swirled in Brenna's gut. Hanging out in public spaces, even with a friend, was stressful. And Lulu was back at her apartment.

Edith slid her purse off her tense shoulder and hung it back on the coatrack. Then she pulled Brenna by the elbow through the swinging doors. A couple of ladies sat drinking coffee and eating pastries. But the person Brenna zeroed in on was Cora, who gave her a little wave.

If she wasn't Owen's mother, Brenna would eagerly share her heart. But she didn't want to put her friend in the middle of anything. She was probably here for a summer camp update, anyway. They greeted with a hug and Edith scurried off to get Brenna a cup of coffee in a to-go cup so it would stay nice and hot.

"I wanted to thank you for the opportunity to co-lead summer camp. It was just what the doctor ordered," Brenna said, a little too much emotion lacing her voice.

The older woman reached across the table and covered Brenna's hand with her own. "Are you okay?" Her deep blue eyes dripped with concern, making Brenna tear up. But she forced the wetness away. She would not cry. She was done with crying and feeling sorry for herself.

Nope. Through the altercation with Bo, she had learned she was strong. She was leaning into that strength, even though she felt more vulnerable now than she had in a while.

"I'm fine." She gave a little nervous laugh. "Bo was scary, not dangerous." She still took delight looking back on that situation because she hadn't panicked. She was hopeful she was on the mend and ready to move forward with her life. And now that Carter had taken her on as a client to handle all of her accounting needs, all she had to do was bake. Carter would handle everything else. "I got two more baking clients," she told Cora, trying to infuse excitement into her voice.

"I'm happy for your baking business, Brenna. But I wanted to know if you were okay with what was happening with Owen." Edith dropped off the coffee and hurried away. The ladies at the other table got up to leave. Other than Edith's off-key humming as she cleaned the glass in the display cases, the bakery was empty.

Brenna swallowed the emotional lump in her throat. She'd stopped by Laney's yesterday in an attempt to pry some information from her, but Owen's sister-in-law had no idea what was happening.

Cora squeezed her hand and gave her a sad

smile. "I thought this time you and Owen would make it to the finish line."

Brenna shook her head. "That won't be happening." She hadn't wanted to allow Owen into her life because she felt so broken after the break-in and assault. She hadn't wanted to saddle anyone with her brokenness. But now that she was feeling stronger, now that those events didn't seem to define her, she wanted a future with Owen. Except he didn't care for her in the same way.

Cora gave a firm shake of her head, her gray curls bouncing with the motion. "I see how Owen looks at you. And you at him. If that isn't love, I don't know what is."

"No. I thought maybe there was something, but not anymore." She must have read too much into their relationship, or maybe it was just that they were working so closely together. Because as soon as he learned she was okay after the Bo incident, Owen didn't seem to have an interest in her. At all.

"Owen is miserable."

"Same here," popped out of her mouth before she could censor her tongue. She probably shouldn't tell Cora how she felt. She didn't want to put the woman in the middle. But frankly, Cora was like a mother to her. And over the past eight months, she'd become a close friend.

"Want to hear what I think?"

Brenna shrugged like she didn't care. But she couldn't wait to hear whatever wisdom Cora had for her. Especially if it unlocked the secret of why Owen was pulling away from her.

"I think he's running scared." Cora took a sip of her iced coffee. "Give him a little time and I bet he'll come around. I have a feeling the two of you will be back together soon."

Running scared? Brenna's back sank against the crossrail of the chair as she contemplated the older woman's words. She'd basically done the same thing to him in high school. But she hadn't had the guts to make a peace offering back then because his career choice had scared her too much. If Cora was right, and Owen decided to come back and ask for a second shot, she'd forgive him for pushing her away.

It was the least she could do after she'd walked out of his life and blocked his calls ten years ago.

And if they got another chance at happily-ever-after, she'd never let him go.

The moment he spotted Brenna's lime-green Jeep pull into Laney's wedding venue drive, nervous tension dropped from Owen's body. The Bo incident had occurred one agonizing week ago. Since then, he'd spent most of his time reflecting and, through prayer, was learning what real humility looked like. Now he'd get a chance to speak with her. Alone. And this time, he'd be honest with her.

But as she neared, he saw the wariness covering her features and his nerves ratcheted up again. Maybe getting her here and being honest with her wouldn't work? He scuffed a hand along the back of his neck, and the prickles where the barber had shaved errant hairs tickled his fingertips. After dropping Evie at his mother's, he'd gone to the barber for a cut and shave because today was special. The outcome of this conversation would define his life. So he planned to do everything in his power to get Brenna to give him another chance.

Brenna pulled her Wrangler into a gravel parking spot and seemed to take forever to emerge.

He hoped she'd give them a second shot at love. Her door opened and Lulu rushed over to him. Owen reached down to scratch her ears. The mini Bernedoodle sat and leaned into the scratches as Brenna walked over. When he stood, Lulu raced off, leaving Brenna on her own.

She stopped in front of him, chin high, looking nothing like the frightened woman he'd reconnected with seven weeks ago. She oozed confidence, and with Lulu off playing, he'd say somewhere along the line she'd overcome her fears. He wanted to pump his fist in victory for her. But one look at her face, and her set chin, sobered him. He had a lot of explaining to do.

She stopped a few feet from him and looked him directly in the eye. "Yes?"

He'd been purposefully vague in the text he'd sent, asking her to come over to Laney's wedding venue to talk. It hadn't taken him long to move into Laney's second-floor, two-bedroom apartment, and Evie had accepted the change of scenery like a trouper. But now it was time to clear the air between him and Brenna—just not in this gravel parking lot.

"I thought we could chat at the gazebo." She frowned at his words, but brushed past him and started along the stepping stone trail to the freshly painted white gazebo lined with twinkle lights. One of the romantic spots Laney's clients used for professional photographs.

Brenna stepped into the covered space, turned and crossed her arms, looking ready for a fight.

The inside of the gazebo was lined with bench seats. He sat across from her. Though she remained standing, he longed for her to loosen up enough to take a seat.

"Thanks for coming over," he said, attempting to break the tense mood. She gave him a tight nod. This wasn't going to be easy, but she was worth it. He could practically taste their bright future, so he plowed forward.

"I'm sorry, Brenna. So sorry." At his apology, her stance relaxed a bit. That slight movement gave him the encouragement he needed to move forward.

"When I heard what was happening on the police scanner with Bo and imagined the danger you were in, it brought me right back to when I lost Willow." She sucked in a breath and dropped to the bench seat across from him, shock covering her pretty features.

"I didn't realize that, Owen." The look on her face had softened, giving him confidence in sharing his heart with her, so he plunged in.

"I've been miserable without you."

"Same here." At her agreeable words, he crossed the four feet between them and settled beside her. At his boldness, her eyes lit up, and right then, he knew he had a chance with her. The sweet aroma of her shampoo enveloped him and he couldn't wait for them to spend lazy weekends and holidays together. As he took her delicate hand in his, hope for the future filled his chest. The feel of her skin against his gave him a rush of adrenaline.

"This sounds selfish," he started, "but I walked away from you out of fear. I was afraid of losing you, so I tried to distance myself." He licked his lips, nervous because his explanation sounded so childish. But in all that drama, his feelings had been so real. So scary. His thoughts and decisions had made so much sense at the time. "I figured if we parted ways, the hurt would go away. But instead, I can't stand being apart from you. I miss you." His pulse raced while he waited for her response.

"I miss you, too." His heart leaped with joy at her declaration. He lifted her hand and smoothed a gentle kiss against her exquisite skin. Then he continued to share his heart with the woman he adored.

"I love you, Brenna." When her face tipped up to his, he took the opportunity and pressed a soft kiss against her lips. It tasted like a promise of forever until she pulled back and shook her head.

"Owen, I need to apologize, too." The look on her face scared him. Had she taken this time apart to realize she enjoyed life more without him?

"For what?" He'd been horrible to her since Wednesday. Unwilling to talk. Being abrupt with her. She had nothing to apologize for. In fact, she had every right to tell him to take off. For good.

"Back in high school, I was scared about your upcoming career in law enforcement, so I blocked your calls." His mouth fell open at her pronouncement.

"What? That makes no sense." Why hadn't she talked with him? Why ghost him?

"I've lived with my parents' disastrous relationship since my father got shot on the job. I swore I'd never marry a police officer." He wanted to smack his palm against his forehead. It all made sense now. How come he'd never considered that as a possibility? She'd gone through a lot with her dysfunctional household, so it made sense she was afraid of something like that happening again.

"You should have talked with me about it."

"See, that's the thing. I knew if I told you there was a chance for us, then you wouldn't follow your dream. And I couldn't have that. I loved you then, and I love you even more now." She wrung her hands in worry, but his pulse quickened at her proclamation of love. "I didn't want you to feel trapped, so I let you go. And I've regretted it ever since." He appreciated her concern for his future. But he'd wanted *her*.

"You didn't trust me."

"Just like you didn't trust God on Wednesday," she responded. Touché.

He grinned and then framed her face with his hands. She was so gorgeous. The sunlight kissed her sparkling eyes, turning them a light blue that he could spend the rest of his days gazing into.

"Let's put all that in the past, shall we?" She

gave him a slight nod and then he pressed his lips to hers, thankful for this second chance that God had given them. After he kissed her, she leaned back and gave him a sweet smile.

"So, tell me all about your baking business," he asked. He was brimming with pride that she'd taken this leap of faith and was now running her own business and doing the work she loved. She filled him in, telling him that right now she wasn't accepting new clients because she wanted to get a feel for the amount of time it would take to fill her weekly orders.

"That's great news." He couldn't help himself from stealing another kiss.

"What about you?" she asked. "Now that camp is over, do you have any idea what you are going to do for a career?" That's right, she didn't know. He had pulled away from her the day Pastor Reed offered him the youth pastor role. He filled her in, and she threw her arms around him.

"Oh, Owen, that's so exciting. I never would have guessed pastor for you, but now that you explain the role, it totally makes sense. You have all those qualities."

His heart lifted that she'd think so highly of him. Well, if she was going to be his wife, he should expect it, but he didn't want to get ahead of himself. He wanted to give them a few months before he popped the question, though there was little doubt in his mind that he wanted to spend the rest of his life with Brenna.

Epilogue

Brenna let out a happy little sigh as she snuggled closer to Owen while the bonfire crackled at their feet. Seemed like a perfect ending to the year—a celebration at the Victory Youth Camp firepit. The place that had brought her and Owen together was the spot where they would close out the year together. With his entire family. As darkness surrounded them, he kissed her forehead, lingering for a moment. She took in the scent of his aftershave, mingled with the smell of smoke, loving everything about the evening.

"How's your baking endeavor coming, Brenna?" Emma asked as she burrowed closer to her husband, Carter. Their triplets were sound asleep in Cora's living room, having a giant cousins sleepover that they'd been looking forward to for weeks.

"Amazing. And I have you to thank," she told her friend. "You were one of the first to hire me to provide baked goods."

"It was an easy ask because your sweets are so, so good."

Wade got up to add wood to the fire. Cora resettled the blanket over her legs, looking entirely satisfied to have all her family in one place. Finally.

Cora had shared about the trials and tribulations they'd had, but God had made things right and now all the adult children were here to stay.

"I'm going to put this sleepy one to bed," Ethan said as he rose with Ava. Laney, hand on her pregnant belly, leaned over to kiss their youngest good night. He grinned at his wife, then headed toward Cora and Wade's front door to settle her with her sisters and cousins in the living room.

The fire crackled with the added wood. Wade kicked the logs around with the poker and then sat next to his wife, taking her hand in his and giving her the most loving look.

"I can't believe it's New Year's Eve," Trisha said, her hand covering her swollen belly. Her husband, Walker, gazed at her like she walked on water. They had such a strong relationship, even though they'd been thrown together to revive an ailing horse farm and raise three orphans together. Now God had blessed them with another, due in March. Their three children were with Emma and Carter's triplets at Memaw's sleepover, apparently a McCaw tradition.

"I know," Owen piped up. His voice sounded funny. Maybe he was coming down with a cold? Brenna wanted to ask him, but didn't want to sound like a mother hen with his family right there. Instead, she enjoyed the warmth from his side. Her heart raced at the notion of having him as a boyfriend again. After the event a year ago, she never thought she'd be able to trust a man. But here she was.

He gazed at her and traced his finger along her cheekbone, the happiness in his eyes filling her with joy. She hoped they'd get a few minutes alone to share a kiss later on.

"And you, taking on that youth pastor role and killing it," Autumn stated. Her husband, Wyatt, held their sleeping one-year-old against his chest. "My friend Caroline says you are doing an admirable job." Brenna took such delight from Owen's sister's kind words. The pastor role had been a hard decision, but the job responsibilities suited Owen well and he always returned from work smiling.

"Oh, she's being too kind," Owen responded, then shifted in the seat as though uncomfortable with the praise. Praise he deserved.

A sound came from the baby monitor beside him. They both looked at it for a moment and breathed a collective sigh of relief when Evie didn't make another noise. She'd been sleeping through the night for a couple of months now. Tonight she was in Owen's old bedroom, but next year, she'd be on the floor in the living room for the cousins sleepover.

"I can't believe she took her first steps yesterday," Brenna whispered. That she'd been there to see the milestone had meant the world to her. Warmth unfurled in her chest at the memory.

"She's unstoppable now." Owen chuckled. A proud smile bloomed on his face.

"It's almost midnight," Ethan said as he returned and settled next to his wife, cuddling close.

Owen stood, lifting his arm from Brenna's shoulders. She missed his touch. He leaned forward and rubbed his hands together as though cold, but the heat emanating from the fire was intense. Warm enough that Brenna was a little sweaty.

Then he dropped to the ground so quickly she thought he'd fallen, but instead he turned and crouched on one knee, a serious expression on his face.

She sucked in a breath.

"Brenna," Owen began, his voice a little shaky. She gave him an encouraging smile and spotted his shoulders straighten with confidence.

"I am so glad we reconnected seven months ago. And that my mother forced us to co-lead camp this summer." Chuckles came from his family, but she only had eyes for Owen. The man of her dreams.

"I love you so much and can't wait to spend the rest of my life with you. Will you marry me? And Evie?"

She looked into his mesmerizing eyes, and her breath caught at the base of her throat. A wife and mother. Two things she thought those horrible men had stolen from her. But instead, she was even stronger than before.

"Yes, oh yes!" She threw her arms around Owen and squeezed tight. As cheers rose from the family, the stubble on his chin tickled her cheek.

"Well, then, Sunshine." At his high school term of endearment for her, she blushed. She recalled the day he'd accidentally used it when they were at the stream. The day he had kissed her for the first time. She finally felt like she'd grown back into that moniker. Sunshine. A happy person. A glass half-full kind of gal. He leaned back and pulled out a jeweler's box from his pocket. "How about we replace that fidget ring with this?"

He slid off the fidget ring she no longer needed and slid on a gorgeous, emerald-cut diamond.

Her stomach flipped in ecstatic little circles. She lifted her hand, and the stone twinkled in the firelight. In the background, his entire family surrounded the bonfire, smiling and taking part in this joyous moment. A story they'd tell Evie one day. And maybe, if God blessed them, other children as well.

"I love it, Owen. It is gorgeous." Her heart pressed against her chest, thudding quickly. *Thank you, God, for healing me and bringing Owen to me right when I needed him. And right when he needed me.*

Then Owen kissed her thoroughly, letting her know how much he loved her.

"It's midnight," someone called out. Owen deepened the kiss and her pulse galloped.

He had always captivated her. And now he was hers. Forever.

Someone yelled out, "Happy New Year!"

She pressed her forehead to his, her gaze on his wide smile, and hoped for many shared New Year's Eves.

* * * * *

Dear Reader,

Brenna and Owen's sweet love story was a joy to write. I especially enjoyed the journey of Owen learning to lean on God while preparing Bible lessons for the campers. It's so easy to get out of the habit of walking closely with God, as Owen did. However, the truth is that resuming the habit is just as simple!

Thank you for joining me on Brenna and Owen's journey in Serenity, Texas, the fifth and final installment of the Triple C Ranch series. I am sad to say goodbye to the McCaw family, but my next miniseries will take place in Serenity as well, so you may see a command performance by some of the McCaw family members!

If you'd like to read Owen and Brenna's extra epilogue—think married and happily-ever-after—please visit my website heidimain.com to download this sweet gem. While there, you can sign up for my newsletter to receive monthly book news, giveaways, life reports as well as deleted scenes and extra epilogues that I now offer with the release of each new book!

Hugs,
Heidi